Fox Hollow

JILLIAN WRIGHT

authorHOUSE®

AuthorHouse™
1663 Liberty Drive
Bloomington, IN 47403
www.authorhouse.com
Phone: 1-800-839-8640

© *2009 Jillian Wright. All rights reserved.*

No part of this book may be reproduced, stored in a retrieval system, or transmitted by any means without the written permission of the author.

First published by AuthorHouse 11/3/2009

ISBN: 978-1-4490-2510-6 (sc)
ISBN: 978-1-4490-2511-3 (hc)

Printed in the United States of America
Bloomington, Indiana

This book is printed on acid-free paper.

Introduction

OUR STORY BEGINS IN SULTRY LOUISIANA IN the 1950's and ends in the early 1960's. Most of the drama occurs at Fox Hollow, a family estate inherited by Dorothy's parents. Dorothy has now inherited the estate, but with one stipulation: she must be the guardian of her mentally ill mother, a mother with whom she has had a stormy relationship. The times are simpler; the story occurs before the use of personal computers and cell phones. Having an illegitimate child was still considered somewhat of a disgrace, and the child's legitimacy depended upon whether the mother was married at the time of the birth.

Nevertheless, some things never change. There have always been dysfunctional families, and in most families, the burden of responsibility falls upon one or two members of the family, making them strong, but also resentful. How can Dorothy expect to have love and marriage while balancing family obligations? She yearns for a love relationship, but with whom? Her childhood sweetheart or her ex-husband?

To complicate the matter is an unsolved murder. What really happened to Aunt Patty?

The fact that the most challenging character is mentally ill is not meant to show disrespect toward persons who suffer form mental illness, but is rather, a reflection of attitudes during those times. And, as we shall see, the most difficult person has some redeeming human qualities.

Chapter 1

LIKE A ROBOT, DOROTHY FOSTER BOARDED THE plane and fastened her seatbelt. Placing her small daughter, Stephanie, on a pillow by the window before buckling the child's belt, she tried to generate some enthusiasm. It was the child's first plane ride. "If you look out the window soon, you'll see fluffy, pink clouds," she pointed out, trying to smile although her face felt frozen.

Normally she was a calm mother, and Stephanie was a happy, placid child. No one might guess that the child had no legitimate father and that she had a mentally ill grandmother. Dorothy had taken pains to raise her child sensibly-free from the constant anxiety she had suffered as a child. Always, Dorothy, the adult, was composed and in control.

But now she was having difficulty remaining calm. For the first time in three years she was to see her father, and he was dying.

She did not even notice the flight attendant's pantomime about emergency exits, cushions, and how to brace one's head for a crash landing. When the woman, clad in orange and blue with a matching smock, mentioned flotation devices, however, Dorothy shuddered and returned to the present.

How would it feel to be in freezing water, tossed about by waves, clinging desperately with numb fingers to the floating cushion from an airplane seat? Stephen's little sister had died in this way when she was just Stephanie's age, except her accidental death was caused by a fall from a boat on a family picnic.

Once in the air and settled with a snack for Stephanie and coffee for herself, Dorothy reread the letter from her father.

"I know you do not want to forgive your mother," her father had written, "but now you must lay personal animosity aside. I have no one else I can trust."

It was true, Dorothy thought. Except for her father, she was the only responsible family member. She was fond of her two younger brothers, but they were both naïve and lacking in judgment. Perhaps she and her father had protected them too much. She could remember little Phillip and Scott coming in from school on the day their mother had been in a catatonic trance, her eyes staring and unknowing, her outstretched arms rigid. Dorothy had met the little boys outside, herding them through crisp autumn leaves to the comfort of a neighbor's home. "Stay here so mother can rest," she had said, and later, after their mother had been hospitalized, Dorothy and her father had let the children think that their mother's illness was a physical one. Philip would be 22 now, just five years younger than Dorothy, and Scott would be just 20. Perhaps they would gain a sense of responsibility when they were more mature.

Dorothy had not come immediately upon receiving her father's letter. Her first impulse was to deny him. She would write, "I'm sorry I can never see you again, but under the circumstances, it is not possible." To go home now would undo all the effort she had taken to preserve her anonymity, her separate and secret identity. She had even changed her name when she moved away. She did not want anyone to know where she lived or where she worked. She did not want her mother to know she had had a baby, and she did not want her child to know there was a grandmother who was evil.

But in the end, love for her father prevailed. She could not deny him his dying wish. It was not his fault her mother was the way she was. If he had used Dorothy, placing too many burdens on her young shoulders, it was because he had nowhere else to turn. He sincerely believed that the family's happiness depended upon the mother's mental health. Thus, his every breath and waking effort had been dedicated to the restoration of his wife's well-being. If only the mother were well and happy could the family hope to be happy. This was her father's obsession. All else was of little importance. Dorothy's own hopes, wishes, and dreams did not count. She was only valued for her contribution to the larger family goal-restoration of the mother's mental health and preservation of the family unit.

Touching her cheek gingerly, Dorothy realized it was wet.

Chapter 2

AT THE GRINDING SOUND OF THE LANDING gear and the feel of the first bump of wheels on the runway, Dorothy's dread increased. Who would meet the plane? Her mother, luckily, did not drive. But would she come along to the airport?

It was with a sense of relief that Dorothy recognized her brother Scott in the airport lobby. She had not seen him since he was seventeen. Now he was accompanied only by a petite redhead, probably not more than 21 years old. This would be Harriet, his bride. The girl had green eyes and a sprinkle of freckles across her nose and uneven teeth, which she displayed in a shy grin. She wore jeans and a beige jersey, sandals with gaily painted toenails. Somehow she did not fit the image Dorothy had been harboring of her. Cousin Malcolm had said she had been a bar waitress, maybe even an exotic dancer. Dorothy and Scott's mother had thrown a fit when Scott had married this girl and had refused to have them in the house.

Dorothy decided she liked her new sister-in-law. True, her brother was too young to be married. He, like Phillip, had not been a good student, and after dropping out of college had drifted from one low-paying job to another. Still, he was appealing in his boyish way, and his young wife, with her lack of ambition and refinement, seemed well suited to him. At least the girl was open and friendly like Scott, who hugged Dorothy and Stephanie with boyish enthusiasm.

Outside, the sticky Louisiana air seemed to close in on them. Once in the car, Stephanie, her cheeks and brow damp and her normally straight hair now curly, promptly fell asleep before Dorothy could even point out to her the grey Spanish moss, hanging mournfully from twisted oaks. The humidity was oppressive. Had she always thought so? The atmosphere reminded Dorothy of the somber reason for her visit.

As though also affected by the humidity, Scott's high spirits seemed to evaporate. His countenance sagged as he began to tell Dorothy about their father's illness and his long hospitalization. He also seemed genuinely puzzled about the troubles he was having with his mother.

"You wouldn't believe the things she said to Harriet!" he said indignantly. "I would never have believed she could act this way."

"I would have believed it," Dorothy said softly. "I should have warned you."

But warning Scott and Phillip had been precisely what Dorothy and her father had never wanted to do. They had always taken care to shield the little boys from any unpleasantness, herding them quickly away to neighbors and friends unless the mother was in a good mood. Phillip and Scott had always believed that their mother was a very sweet lady who was in delicate health and was sometimes a little nervous. They could never conceive of her capacity for malicious mischief and they could never fully understand why Dorothy had wanted to move away and sever all ties with her family.

But now Phillip and Scott were no longer children. They must learn to accept reality in order to defend themselves. Soon they would no longer have their father to protect their interests.

To Harriet, Dorothy said, "Our mother is so sick she is dangerous. You must never trust her. You must never believe a single word she says."

"Oh no," Harriet and Scott answered, almost in unison. "She isn't that bad! Most of the time she makes good sense. It's just that she didn't want us to get married."

"Paranoid schizophrenics always do make sense," said Dorothy, quoting a psychiatrist from the long-ago unhappy past. "They learn to defend their ideas in a logical way. It's just that their original hypotheses are misconceived, having been based on faulty perception."

This last bit of information seemed more than either Scott or Harriet wanted to learn or were willing to digest. Their very innocence made Dorothy more determined than ever to protect them.

"Don't let her ruin your marriage," she cautioned, "like the way she destroyed mine."

As they turned into a tree-lined street, Dorothy recognized the pleasant, middle-class neighborhood where she had grown up. Now her brother Phillip inhabited the grey stucco house, which seemed to blend in with the Spanish moss in the trees. The parents had inherited Fox Hollow, Aunt Patty's and Uncle Arthur's estate in the country, and after moving there, had given Phillip the old house.

Phillip and his wife Carlotta were supposed to take care of Stephanie while Dorothy went to the hospital to see her father and eventually, on to the estate. Not knowing what mood her mother would be in, Dorothy had not wanted to take her child to her parents' home. She had considered getting a babysitter in Arizona, but she and her daughter were very close. They had never been separated for more than a few hours. She did not want to leave Stephanie in Arizona while she stayed in Louisiana for-how long?

She did not know.

It was Cousin Malcolm who had suggested calling her brother Phillip. Phillip and Carlotta had a baby younger than Stephanie, and they had a woman to help with child care. They could keep Stephanie in the nursery with their child, where she could still see her mother at least once each day.

After meeting Carlotta, Dorothy had second thoughts. Carlotta, not Harriet, was a person who looked like a stripper. Tall and full-figured, she had obviously-dyed black hair, which gave her face a harsh quality. She seemed older than Phillip. In a brazen way, she was pretty, but her mouth was sullen and pouting, not smiling and friendly like Harriet's. Yet her background was supposed to be more respectable than Harriet's. She had met Phillip through people of their own social class.

Perplexed, Dorothy tried to shake off her bad impression of Carlotta. She did not want to be suspicious and critical of everyone like her mother had always been. Dorothy sensed that Carlotta was not overjoyed to have another child to look after, but Phillip was so affable and eager to keep Stephanie that she could not refuse.

After all, she couldn't take a baby to the hospital, could she? So, the sleepy Stephanie was tucked into bed at Phillip's house, and she, Scott and Harriet went on to the hospital, a stark, white building downtown.

Once inside the antiseptic-smelling elevator, Dorothy's eyes swelled with tears. How often in three years had she missed her family! And how could she have ignored her father's goodness? It had been wrong of her to ignore him and her brothers just because she no longer wanted to endure her mother. Because of her mother, she had rejected them all. Now walking down the stark corridor toward room 314, she saw a light on over her father's door. The meaning did not register immediately with Dorothy's conscious mind, even while she could hear herself saying, "None of the other rooms have a light turned on over the door."

Inside the room, they saw that the bedding had been stripped, leaving the hospital mattress bare! They were too late.

Chapter 3

The funeral was over and the will had been read. The true terms of the will were not fully disclosed. The wording had been tactful to avoid hurting the mother. Nevertheless, she had been somewhat miffed. "Why couldn't I handle my own estate?" she had demanded. The lawyers, friends of her father, had soothed and cajoled her.

Over twenty-seven and three quarter million dollars had been left to the mother in a trust, but Dorothy was executor of the estate. She was in control of how the money would be spent. The true meaning of this provision had been revealed to Dorothy in another letter from her father, received that last dreadful day at the hospital.

Not wanting to believe what the empty room meant, Dorothy and Scott had demanded to know where their father was. "Downstairs, downstairs," the young nurse's aide had stammered, as she removed the last bundle of linen from their sight. She had not wanted to say, "Downstairs in the morgue." Someone then steered Dorothy to the nurses' station where the nurse in authority had thrust a plastic bag into her hands. Her father's watch, his ring and his wallet had been neatly wrapped in plastic and sealed. That was all that remained of him.

Also, in the plastic bag was a white envelope with Dorothy's name on it.

Why hadn't she come in time? Why had she procrastinated so long? It was her cousin Malcolm who had finally persuaded her to come at all. He was now driving her car east, having persuaded her to take a plane in order to see her father more quickly. But she had not been quick enough.

In the waiting room she had read the letter through her tears. "I know your mother is hard to get along with," he had written "Her illness makes her vulnerable; so many people reject her. Who will take care of her when I am gone? People will not understand that she cannot help herself." Dorothy closed her eyes. What did it matter if her mother could "help" her behavior? The behavior was still hard to live with! But even in death, her father protected her mother.

"If she has a large amount of money at her disposal, she will be better accepted. People are kinder to someone with money. That is a fact of life. But someone also needs to see that the money is not lost through poor judgment. It must last her all of her life. If she should need hospitalization again, should she show signs of not coping with life, you, Dorothy, can use the money to get her the best hospital treatment. You have always been the most stable and responsible of the children. When your mother dies, you will get one-half of what is left. Scott and Phillip should each get one-fourth. The larger share should be yours for watching over your mother's welfare and estate, for seeing that she is always cared for."

It isn't fair, Dorothy thought. Even in death, her father expected too much. Most people would be thrilled to be in control of so much money! Even though the money was to be spent for her mother's welfare, an unscrupulous person could live very well as the mother's companion, housekeeper, overseer, secretary, or whatever title one chose. But Dorothy did not want this life. She would not live with her mother permanently and pay herself a big salary. She had a good job in Arizona. Her salary was adequate for her needs and Stephanie's. She enjoyed her work as an accountant. She did not want to live in close proximity to her mother. Her brothers would just have to look after family affairs here and she would return to Arizona.

What happened later was somewhat vague. After signing necessary forms at the hospital, she and Scott and Harriet had gone back to Phillip's house. From there, they had all gone to the country estate, leaving the children behind with the nursemaid who worked for Phillip and Carlotta.

Ordinarily, Dorothy would have been thrilled at the sight of the faded black and white sign at the entrance to Fox Hollow. When her uncle and aunt had owned the estate, it had been a haven for Dorothy. Fox Hollow was not the traditional Southern mansion with formal colonial pillars. Instead, it was a somewhat ungainly, three-story white frame structure with wide functional porches on three sides. Nestled on ten acres and surrounded by magnolias and moss-covered oaks, it had a horse pasture in front. The back yard sloped gently to a bayou, which bordered the property.

They were met by a sour-faced woman, Mrs. Crouch, the housekeeper. She led them into the darkened suite where Alicia lay.

Alicia! Although well past middle age, she had the appearance of a young girl. Strawberry blonde curls clung to her damp forehead, surrounding an unlined face with milk-white complexion. Wide, china-blue eyes gave an impression of innocence, which was deceiving, Dorothy thought. Her frothy, pink negligee was adorned with embroidered rosebuds and satin ribbons. The total image of Alicia had not changed since Dorothy had seen her last.

"How nice of you to come, Dorothy," she said sweetly, as though it had only been yesterday since they had met. "Let's have some tea."

Somehow the boys had mustered the strength to tell their mother the news. What they had dreaded had happened. Their father, Alicia's husband, was dead. Their wives, still in disfavor with Alicia, stayed tactfully in the background.

In those first few hours, Alicia showed amazing inner strength. The delicate hot-house flower whom her father had always sought to nurture had an inner core of steel. With grudging admiration, Dorothy watched her mother direct funeral arrangements with calmness and determination. By bedtime all details were settled.

By morning, however, Alicia had lapsed into emotional shock. The housekeeper who carried her breakfast tray found Alicia mute and staring. The doctor advised them all to wait and see. Sometimes such cases recovered within a day or two after a trauma. Certainly Alicia had had such spells before. Mrs. Crouch would help them sit with her.

On the morning that the funeral was to take place, Cousin Malcolm arrived. Crushing Dorothy to him in a bear-like grip, he pressed his lips hard against hers. Malcolm was definitely a kissing cousin.

Chapter 4

MALCOLM HAD COME INTO DOROTHY'S LIFE AGAIN only a few weeks ago. For the second time, she was in love with him. The first affair had been twelve years earlier and in this very house.

Fox Hollow, as an estate, was not at all pretentious. How well it had suited Aunt Patty and Uncle Arthur when they had lived here! Uncle Arthur, her father's only brother, was ten years his senior and was a quiet and unassuming man. The acquisition of money had never changed his personality. Dorothy's father had earned a comfortable living as a professional architect, but most of his energy had been diverted to the maintenance of his family. Uncle Arthur, on the other hand, had never had children. Because they had no descendents, he and Patty had left their fortune acquired from the shipping industry to Dorothy's father.

Dorothy had heard about their deaths from her brothers. Uncle Arthur died first, about the time that Stephanie was born. Aunt Patty had died a year later. Dorothy had sent flowers and regretted she could not do more. She had dearly loved her aunt and uncle.

When Dorothy was a child, she had thought of Aunt Patty as Mrs. Santa Claus. Aunt Patty must always have been grey-headed. Although her hair style was as unpretentious as the cotton housedress which covered her short and rather dumpy shape, her plump pink face had radiated good will. Possibly her cheeks were flushed from leaning over steaming pots in the kitchen.

Dorothy's mouth had always watered at the thought of hot buttered popcorn, homemade ice cream, fudge and gingerbread that came from Aunt Patty's kitchen, but this was not the best part of her childhood visits. The best part about Fox Hollow was that here she could be a child. She could lie in Aunt Patty's guest bed in the sewing room late in the morning and look at the pink roses on the wallpaper. She did not have to worry whether or not the little boys had been fed. Aunt Patty would have seen to that.

Once outside, the child Dorothy could play on one of the wide porches. She never played near the bayou because of water moccasins, but stayed a little distance away, sometimes swinging in the rope hammock, strung between two oaks.

Inside the house, the halls were as wide as rooms in most houses. From the front hall, one turned right into the double living room, a front parlor and a back parlor separated by glass doors. Leaded glass windows were on three sides. To the left was the dining room with an enormous but rather plain glass chandelier and a built-in china closet in the corner. The room was functional rather than elegant. The floors were oak and were kept bare. For some reason, Aunt Patty didn't like rugs. A massive staircase, also not carpeted, opened into the front hall. The stairs were neither graceful nor winding but turned into almost a square with three landings. The upstairs hall was also a rectangle and overlooked the downstairs stairwell on three sides. Mahogany-stained oak had been used for the staircase. It had once taken Dorothy an hour to dust all the banisters for her aunt.

At the back of the house was the kitchen. A second staircase, cramped and winding and painted apple green, came from the upstairs hall into the pantry which adjoined the kitchen. It was here that Malcolm encountered Dorothy the summer she was fifteen.

At fifteen, she had never had a boyfriend. She had been too busy at home. Most of the time, she had hurried straight home from school. Her mother might be ill and need her, and when or if her mother was in the hospital, someone needed to keep the little brothers after school. Someone needed to wash clothes or start supper, and that "someone" was usually Dorothy. She also had her homework to do. At fifteen, she was a straight "A" student, but because she hadn't lingered with the other kids after school, some of them thought she was unfriendly. Their accusations made her more shy than ever.

She also thought she wasn't pretty. At fifteen, her ideal image of beauty was to be blonde and delicate, with slender fingers and tiny feet. Instead, Dorothy was moderately tall and large-boned, with generous-sized (it seemed to her) hands and feet. Her hair was straight. Although not fat, she was more sturdy than frail. She felt there was no hope for her. She would never have sex appeal.

That summer her mother was still in the hospital and her father had sent her with her brothers for a visit to Fox Hollow. Aunt Patty had especially wanted Dorothy to come and help entertain her young nephew, who had come to live at Fox Hollow following his parents' death in a car accident. Because he was Aunt Patty's nephew, he was Dorothy's cousin only by marriage.

At seventeen, Malcolm had been as large as a grown man. His thick black hair was combed, with help of hair oil, into a pompadour, as was the style. Liquid velvet brown eyes were sometimes languid and bored, sometimes challenging and provocative beneath thick, straight lashes. His jaw was a little too heavy to be handsome, but on him it was perfect, Dorothy decided. Upon occasion, the shape of his mouth had a sardonic look, but when he smiled, this illusion was instantly dispelled. And he did not think Dorothy was ugly.

Catching her on the back stairs and pushing her up against the cupboard, he had said, "You and I are kissing cousins."

From that time on, Dorothy could not approach the pantry or back staircase without simultaneously dreading and hoping that Malcolm would be there.

Chapter 5

Now arm-in arm Malcolm and Dorothy strolled up the walk to the wide veranda of Fox Hollow.

"It's good to be home-just like old times," Malcolm whispered gently, giving her a meaningful nudge and squeeze. She knew he remembered the back staircase and pantry.

But it was not like old times. Fox Hollow was no longer the blissful haven of her childhood. Instead of Aunt Patty in the kitchen baking gingerbread, the sour-faced Mrs. Crouch now doled out frugal portions of nutritious but unappetizing fare. And the true mistress of Fox Hollow was now a mad woman, her mother, her enemy. The little boys no longer played barefoot on the lawn or fished in the bayou, but stood stiffly about in their grown-up clothes. And, Dorothy did not know what to make of their wives. Were they friends or enemies? Worst of all, no longer would her beloved father come down the long circular drive to fetch the children at Fox Hollow. Today he would be buried.

The contrast of past and present was too much to bear. Why couldn't life stay always the same, suspended in time? Dorothy shivered in the sunshine even as she perspired.

Even Malcolm was not the same. Although he had only lived in Arizona a few short weeks, one would never guess it from his appearance. He had gone totally western. Already he had acquired a healthy-looking tan, which suited him and went well with his thick, dark, blown-dry hair-no longer greasy with hair oil as it had been when he was a teen. The liquid brown eyes had not changed, but around his slightly too-thick neck hung a string of turquoise and silver Indian beads. His muscular chest and shoulders were shown off well in a western shirt. A typical Arizona tourist, Dorothy thought, partially in admiration but more in exasperation. He did look handsome but his attire was totally out of place in this setting, especially on this occasion.

Once inside the formal front parlor, Malcolm seemed even more out of place. The brothers and sisters-in-law sat stiffly in their chairs. Carlotta alone seemed impressed by Malcolm's appearance. Usually sullen and bored, she now became more animated-almost vivacious.

"Don't I get a kiss, Malcolm, or am I not a kissing cousin,?" she demanded, affecting gaiety. Without much enthusiasm, it seemed, Malcolm kissed her brusquely. He was a little more eager to kiss Harriet, who appeared shy and hung back.

Upon hearing that Dorothy's mother was in a catatonic state, Malcolm demanded, "Why haven't you done more to help her?"

"She's being watched over by Mrs. Crouch," Dorothy answered defensively. "The doctor said to wait and see if she would recover by herself."

"But it's been two days," Malcolm protested. "She should be in expert hands. Dorothy, your father would expect more from you."

"If you mean a sanitarium, we could scarcely commit her before the funeral," Dorothy snapped. "We had some other things on our minds!"

"Of course, Darling, I'm sorry I was critical." Malcolm soothed, putting his arms around her. "It's all right. You did all you could. But after the funeral, we must get her more help. Your father would want that."

Resting her head on Malcolm's shoulder, Dorothy could see Carlotta's face out of the corner of her eye. Her expression was absolutely venomous.

"Miss Dorothy, you must come upstairs," Mrs. Crouch interrupted. "Miss Alicia-she is awake and she wants to go to the funeral."

Chapter 6

Dorothy's mother had recovered from her temporary episode as the doctor had predicted and had been able to attend the funeral and the reading of the will three days later. The temporary crisis had been averted. The delicate flower had inner strength once more. Alicia did not need to be hospitalized immediately. However, long range plans for her care which took into account her precarious mental health should be made, Dorothy realized.

Alicia's return to sanity only intensified Dorothy's negative attitude about her mother. Their first fight was about Dorothy's child.

"Carlotta told me you left your daughter at her house. I suppose you were ashamed for me to see her," Alicia had said, when Dorothy brought the breakfast tray. Sitting up in her four-poster bed, she was once more the queen in a satin bed jacket, surveying her kingdom. "Darling, you know I would forgive you," she chided, attempting to put her arm around Dorothy, who shrank away. Alicia had decided to take a motherly and forgiving attitude toward Dorothy.

"Darling, whose baby is it? Who did you have an affair with? I don't approve but I forgive you. That dull Stephen you married couldn't have been too exciting. I can't say that I blame you for running after somebody else. Was that why Stephen left you? Did he find out? Tell me," she begged.

At first, Alicia refused to believe that Stephanie was Stephen's child. Her attitude began to change from one of motherly forgiveness to one of a person wronged. One of Alicia's tricks was to accuse others of duplicity, which she herself practiced. "Of course you would say it was your husband's child. You would be ashamed to say otherwise. I always told your father you were sneaky. I don't know why he put you in charge of my money. You needn't think you are going to stop me if I want to spend something. But he thought you were responsible. I don't call it responsible to have a bastard child. But like I told your father, 'You mustn't blame Dorothy if she runs after men. Plain girls need to.' In my case, I never needed to run after men. I had the looks men liked. The men chased me, not vice-versa," she ended on a note of triumph.

How the conversation could have traveled from Dorothy's child to Alicia's looks and popularity in such a short time was too much for Dorothy to digest. Nor could she answer all her mother's questions at once, so she fled, down the back staircase to the pantry. She longed for Malcolm's waiting arms. He would make her feel attractive. He would prove she did not repel men as her mother had hinted.

But the pantry, now dingy, was desolate and bare. She found Malcolm eating breakfast on the back screened porch off the kitchen.

"That Mrs. Crouch sure knows how to burn toast," he grumbled, laying down his morning paper.

"Be glad she didn't give you wheat germ," Dorothy countered, mustering a faint smile. In a more subdued tone, she relayed her morning's conversation with her mother. "She is the most impossible woman I've ever met," Dorothy sighed. "She hasn't changed a bit."

"But Darling, don't you see?" Malcolm gripped her hand. "She has changed for the worse since your father died. Her conversation proves she isn't in touch with reality. She needs help. And only you can see that she gets it," he insisted.

"I'm not the person to make that decision," Dorothy countered, "because I don't get along with her. I might be tempted to act outside her interest. The only decent thing for me to do is to legally give my guardianship responsibilities to Phillip or Scott. They can be more objective about how the money should be spent and they can decide if Alicia needs help."

Malcolm grasped her hand so hard it hurt. "You must not go against your father's wishes. He told me himself he wanted you in charge. You know your brothers are not responsible. You and your father always kept them from your mother when she was having a spell. They wouldn't recognize her symptoms until it was too late to get help."

Grudgingly, Dorothy agreed. Scott and Phillip were always broke and out of work. Possibly, they would misuse Alicia's money. They would mean no harm but they lacked judgment. They might make unwise investments. Furthermore, their wives did not get along with Alicia. Probably neither of the women her brothers had married would be able to help Alicia in a crisis.

"Oh, Malcolm, what shall I do? I want to go back to Arizona, but I suppose I could get my firm to transfer me to Baton Rouge. I won't live at Fox Hollow, though. If I have to move back here, Stephanie and I will have our own apartment. I will have my career and just check on Mother every few days."

"I knew I could count on you to do what's right," Malcolm said softly. "Your father would be proud of you. Next week I'll help you find an apartment. For now, you need to stay here and watch your mother. Who knows? She may need more specialized help sooner than you think."

Later in the day, Dorothy drove to her brother's house to see Stephanie. Although the little girl missed her mother, she had been happy enough to play with her baby cousin under the watchful eye of the motherly-looking nursemaid.

Carlotta, since the funeral, had spent all her time at Fox Hollow, seemingly trying to ingratiate herself with Alicia. Dorothy wondered why Carlotta wanted to be away from her baby so much, but she felt it was kind of Carlotta to be so concerned for Alicia, especially since Alicia had never been particularly nice to Carlotta. Toward Dorothy, however, Carlotta had been barely civil. Her hostility had seemed to increase since Malcolm's arrival. Perhaps Carlotta thought that his open show of affection for Dorothy was inappropriate when there had been a death in the family. Had Phillip not been so kind and the nurse so warm and friendly, Dorothy would have been inclined to move Stephanie from Carlotta and Phillip's home. But she did not want Stephanie to be at Fox Hollow either. Carlotta's house seemed the lesser of two evils.

"I know Mrs. Deveroux has been gone quite a bit more since our father died, Mrs. Williams," said Dorothy. "I hope it doesn't make Baby Sara lonely."

"Just call me Mattie," the nursemaid said. "Miss Deveroux-she's gone all the time. This death don't make no difference. But me and Sara-we get on fine by ourselves," she added. Dorothy knew that Mattie could tell more but wouldn't. "We're glad to have someone to play with," she added politely.

Both children did seem to get on well with Mattie, and Dorothy was somewhat relieved that Stephanie was in her care and not Carlotta's. Evidently Carlotta was the type who led an active social life. Once again, Dorothy had the feeling that the nursemaid knew more than she was willing to say.

Sitting beside Mattie for a while, Dorothy watched the little girls play. Stephanie, at almost three, had blonde hair like her father and brown eyes like both her parents. In Arizona, Stephanie's blonde hair had been straight and coarse like Dorothy's dark hair, but in the humidity of this climate, the child's hair had begun to curl. More like her father's side of the family, Dorothy thought with a pang. Fox Hollow was only a few miles from where her former mother-in-law had lived.

Phillip and Carlotta's baby, on the other hand, a beautiful plump child just beginning to walk, was dark like Carlotta. Although she did not look like Phillip, who had sandy hair and blue eyes, Dorothy could see a family resemblance. Perhaps she looked like her grandfather. Dorothy wasn't sure. Happily, the little girl seemed to have a sweeter disposition than her mother had.

Soon it was time to return to Fox Hollow for dinner. Dorothy knew that both her brothers and their wives were supposed to be there.

Chapter 7

Coming up the steps onto the wide veranda, Dorothy encountered her brother Scott and his wife Harriet. The red-haired girl had burst through the front door and not said a word to Dorothy. The rims of her eyes were as red as her hair. Scott followed at her heels, looking distressed.

"Aren't you staying to dinner?" Dorothy asked, grabbing her brother's sleeve.

"No!" he said shortly, shrugging her off.

Harriet stopped in her tracks and stopped to look at Dorothy. "You were right about your mother. I don't care if I never see her again!"

Then they went on. Perplexed, Dorothy went inside where the family was already seated for dinner.

At the head of the table sat Alicia, always the queen bee. With reluctant admiration, Dorothy thought her mother looked well in a pale blue taffeta dress with a beaded jacket. Alicia was never in style; somehow, her clothes were always remnants of another era, just as her thoughts and words were often from a world inhabited only by herself. Yet her dress was regal, which made it compatible with her need to preside over every occasion she attended. Only a faint odor of mothballs gave a clue that Alicia's dress, like her personality, was not really in harmony with modern times.

Slipping into her place at the table, Dorothy looked at Carlotta. Generally, Harriet was the more pleasant and placid of the sisters-in-law, but now Harriet had stormed out and Carlotta, by contrast, was almost purring as she sat between Malcolm and Alicia. Phillip, as always, was quiet and noncommittal. No doubt Alicia had said something to hurt Harriet's feelings. Why, oh why, couldn't her mother behave herself like other people? Why must she always be stirring up trouble in the family?

"What was wrong with Harriet and Scott?" Dorothy ventured to ask.

"Oh, that girl is so emotional and unstable," Alicia said with an innocent laugh. "She flies off the handle about every little thing. Scott should never have married her."

"Mother said something about Harriet's having been a cocktail waitress," Phillip interjected dryly.

"Well, if she's that ashamed of it, why did she do it?" Alicia countered. "At least I didn't talk about her topless dancing. People shouldn't do things they are ashamed of," she added self-righteously. "It isn't my fault if other people behave in ways that give them a bad conscience," she continued, looking pointedly at Dorothy, "like having an illegitimate child." An embarrassed hush fell over the table, but Alicia, undaunted, prattled on. "People around here are forever doing bad things and then they act like it's my fault! I didn't do any of those things!"

"If you are talking about me, my daughter is my ex-husband's, and it was your fault he didn't stay around until she was born," Dorothy snapped.

"Why, Dorothy, whatever are you talking about? If Stephen was the father of your baby," she paused, emphasizing the 'if,' "then he was rotten to leave you and you're well rid of him. I don't know what I might have done to run him off, but if I did do something, I'm glad. Any man who would leave his pregnant wife isn't worth having, isn't that right?" She then turned to address Malcolm and Carlotta. "Dorothy should be grateful to me, not petty and childish, don't you think?"

The anger inside Dorothy rose to her throat, causing a wave of nausea to sweep through her. The palms of her hands perspired into the napkin she was clutching. She could understand why most murders occurred within families. How typical of her mother to summarize all of Dorothy's pain into neat cliché's, and how like her mother to inflict harm and then blame her victim! But Dorothy was more mature than the young girl, Harriet. She would not let the others see her lose control.

"I will not dignify your comments with an answer," she said evenly, gazing directly into her mother's china-blue eyes, eyes without compassion or depth. "I consider the topic closed."

Turning to Carlotta, Dorothy then began to talk about Baby Sara and how both the little girls seemed to like Mattie, the nursemaid. For once, Carlotta appeared agreeable and friendly.

Alicia, on the other hand, was beginning to pout. She did not like to be cut off before she was finished with one of her acts. She had no doubt wanted to humiliate Dorothy some more. Tears were beginning to well, and another emotional storm was about to erupt.

"My husband is dead and my daughter is unkind to me," she began with trembling lips. "Most daughters would be kinder to a sick mother who is in mourning." By this time tears were trickling down Alicia's cheeks. With a pang, Dorothy was reminded of her mother's loss. Bad as she was, Alicia had been devoted to her husband.

This time Malcolm came to the rescue. Patting Alicia's hand, he boomed in a jovial voice, "Come on now, Aunt Alicia, let's have some nice hot tea. I'll save Mrs. Crouch the effort and bring it for you myself."

As always, Alicia was more responsive to a male touch. Her husband had been able to avert many unpleasant scenes by cajoling her. She wiped her eyes and smiled weakly. Alicia was the only one in the family who liked hot tea with her meal, although Aunt Patty had also liked it, Dorothy recalled.

When Malcolm returned from the kitchen with the steaming cup, Alicia sipped it and made a face. "Mrs. Crouch, come here," she demanded shrilly.

When the housekeeper appeared, Alicia scolded, "I don't know what possessed you to sweeten my tea. You know I don't like it sugared! Take it back this minute!"

"No, no, Aunt Alicia," Malcolm argued, patiently, as with a child. "I poured this up for you myself. Here, I'll taste it myself to prove it's not sweet."

"Don't do it!" gasped Mrs. Crouch. "I'll just get another cup. Remember that other time?"

"Nonsense, Mrs. Crouch," Malcolm answered coldly, "there's nothing wrong with this tea." He sipped it.

"It isn't sweet, Aunt Alicia; you're just imagining things. You've had a lot of stress on you. You know how you imagine things sometimes, Aunt Alicia."

"I don't believe you," Alicia snapped, jerking the cup from Malcolm and shoving it toward Dorothy. "You are just trying to protect Mrs. Crouch! You taste it, Dorothy."

Dorothy's mind flew back to another time-when she was nine years old. She and her parents and the little brothers had been vacationing at a resort. It was one of the few happy times when all of the family was together. She remembered how pretty her mother looked in a yellow sundress to match her fluffy, yellow hair, and how gay and carefree the mother had seemed those few days at the lake. She had been sincerely sweet to the children, playing with them on the sandy shore, taking an interest in how they could swim. Dorothy also remembered her father, relaxed and tan, pulling the oars in a rowboat to give the children a ride. Whenever his wife was symptom-free, he was happy. They could have passed for any normal, healthy family.

But it could not last. On the way home, they had stopped at a roadside café, one of those family establishments with gaudy windmills and tacky pictures, which amused the children. Dorothy was not sure if her parents had been quarrelling or not, but she noticed that her mother had become increasingly petulant, and uneasiness stirred within her. Even at nine, she could sense a storm brewing. They had been happy for a few days, so now they must pay in emotional pain.

When Alicia's tea had been served, she had tasted it with a grimace. Immediately, she called back the waitress, a homely, pimply-faced girl about seventeen.

"Why did you sugar this tea?" she demanded. "I asked for unsweetened."

"I didn't," stammered the girl. "It is unsweetened."

If the girl had been more experienced, she would have taken the tea away promptly and brought another cup of the same. But being young and not terribly bright, the waitress had continued to insist that the tea was not sweet.

In exasperation, Alicia had shoved the cup toward Dorothy. "You taste it, Dorothy, and tell her it is sweet!" Dorothy had dutifully bent her head and sipped the warm liquid. It was not sweet.

With a child's candor, she had blurted out, "It' really isn't sweet, Mama." The pimply-faced girl smirked with relief.

In a flash, Dorothy knew she had done wrong. The fires in her mother's eyes blazed with hatred. "Someday, Dorothy," she had said venomously, "You will learn to respect your mother. Family loyalty is a trait you need to acquire."

Dorothy had been too upset to finish her meal. Later, she had asked her grim-faced father, "Should I have lied, Daddy? Should I have said the tea was sweet?"

Sadly, he had explained, "Distorted perception in taste and smell is part of your mother's problem. When she thinks she tastes or smells something, she really believes it. So it's best to humor her when she gets like that."

Years later, Dorothy wondered if her father's constant "humoring" had not reinforced the mother's faulty perceptions. Dorothy would not humor her mother. Yet, she was too weary for another round of battle. She was no longer a child of nine. She would not play the teacup game.

"I don't want to taste it," she said, pushing the cup back toward her mother.

"Why not? Just take a little sip," Alicia insisted.

"Miss Alicia, you should be ashamed," the housekeeper burst out. "Don't you remember that other time?"

"Don't taste it," she said to Dorothy.

In amazement, Dorothy gaped at Mrs. Crouch. How dare the housekeeper scold her mistress! Yet Alicia tolerated it. The tears welled up once more in Alicia's eyes. "Maybe you're right. I should be ashamed to make such a fuss over little things," she said meekly, her lower lip trembling. Dorothy could not believe her eyes and ears. Alicia had never been contrite before.

Suddenly, Carlotta did something to surprise them all. Leaning across Alicia, she lifted the teacup and took a generous sip. Mrs. Crouch shuddered.

"You are absolutely right, Alicia, and they are wrong," she announced with supreme confidence. "This cup of tea has definitely been sweetened."

For a moment, Malcolm's face darkened, as Carlotta beamed triumphantly at him. Alicia's face was a mixture of bewilderment and gratitude. Mrs. Crouch had fled the scene in haste.

Malcolm's dark look had been only transitory. Once more, his face became a mask of affability. Offering his arm to Alicia, he said gallantly, "Let's call off our feud about tea and go sit on the porch, shall we?"

Carlotta and Phillip rose and readied themselves to go home. In her new agreeable state of mind, Carlotta promised Dorothy to take good care of Stephanie until Dorothy could come for her the next day.

Dorothy was alone with the dirty dishes. What had caused Carlotta's improved disposition? And what had been her motive for lying about the tea since both Malcolm and Mrs. Crouch had convinced Alicia that she was mistaken? To irritate Malcolm? Or, perhaps to ingratiate herself with Alicia? Carlotta seemed to be working overtime lately to have better relations with her mother-in-law. Perhaps she was genuinely sorry for Alicia and wanted to be kind. Dorothy scolded herself for questioning Carlotta's motives. She must not develop a suspicious nature like her mother's.

The offending teacup remained, half full, in the center of the table. Glancing about to be sure she was alone, Dorothy lifted it to her lips. The tea was sweet.

Chapter 8

In bewilderment Dorothy retreated to her room, Aunt Patty's old sewing room. She did not want to see any more family members. The tea she had tasted was definitely sugared, or was she the one who was going crazy? Perhaps Stephen's mother had been right when she had predicted that the curse of the mother would be passed on to the daughter.

Abruptly she stopped at the door. Mrs. Crouch was in Dorothy's room, holding a piece of paper over the pillow. The woman's little dried-up face, with worried furrows on her brow, reminded Dorothy of a prune. She was not someone Dorothy felt kindly toward, especially not tonight.

"What are you doing?" Dorothy demanded. The housekeeper jumped back slightly, her brow still wrinkled under her mouse-colored hair.

"Oh, Miss Dorothy, I found this on your pillow," the woman said in an agitated voice.

On a piece of lined notebook paper, words had been printed in crayon. Each letter was a different color: red, blue, yellow, green, gold, violet, pink, and reddish brown. It said, "If you are as smart as you think you are, you will go back to Arizona before something happens." A feeling of anger at such childishness flooded Dorothy. Obviously, Mrs. Crouch didn't like her routine disturbed. She wanted Dorothy and the others away so she could run the household unencumbered by guests. Moreover, oddly enough, she seemed to actually have control over Alicia.

"Mrs. Crouch, now that I have caught you in the act of leaving that ridiculous note, why did you write it? Why do you want me gone?"

"Oh no, Miss Dorothy, I don't want you gone. I'm glad you're here. I was just checking the rooms and this note was here already."

"Isn't it strange you would check the rooms in the evenings? Isn't morning a better time to straighten up?"

The housekeeper drew herself up with dignity. "As a matter of fact, I was uneasy that someone might harm you."

The woman seemed sincere enough, but Dorothy was not convinced.

"Mrs. Crouch, why were you so upset when my mother made a fuss about the tea at supper? Surely you're used to her moods by now."

A closed, more guarded look came over the housekeeper's face. "There was another time your mother made a fuss over tea-and that was the day Miss Patty died. That's all."

"But what about the tea?" Dorothy persisted. "What does tea have to do with Patty's death?" Abruptly, the housekeeper handed Dorothy the note.

"Miss Dorothy, your mother is a wicked woman. I'm sure it was she that sent you this." She turned on her heel, leaving Dorothy alone.

Dorothy stood, in the middle of the room, holding the paper. Was her mother this far gone? Only a crazy person would write this childish message. Yet, writing notes had never been her mother's style. If Alicia didn't like something, she usually let the whole world know. Obnoxious as she was, she had never been shy about expressing her feelings. Alicia, if anything, was too straightforward. Subtleness was not one of her traits. Yet with an unstable person, who could be sure? Could anyone predict what Alicia might be capable of? And, Alicia had been upset to think that Dorothy was in charge of her income.

A minute ago, Dorothy had been so certain that Mrs. Crouch was the note-writing culprit. Now she didn't know.

A few minutes earlier, Dorothy had been ready to collapse into bed. Now she had renewed strength. She must find Malcolm and talk to him. Looking down the hall, she noticed that her mother had come upstairs and was watching television in her bedroom. Happily, the door was nearly closed and she would not see Dorothy and accost her on the way downstairs. In the kitchen, Dorothy could hear Mrs. Crouch noisily washing pots and pans. She went outside where she found Malcolm sitting alone in the old-fashioned porch swing on the side veranda. The gentle refreshing breeze felt cool on her perspiring brow. The honeysuckle and wisteria gave off a sweet odor, and the crickets chirped steadily. The setting implied a tranquility Dorothy could not feel.

"It's about time you came," Malcolm said, pulling her down beside him. "I've been wondering why you were avoiding me."

"You seemed to be getting enough female attention from Mother and Carlotta at the dinner table," she retorted. "I've had enough of all of them."

He looked at her sharply. "I can't stand Carlotta, but I'm nice to her for your brother's sake. And I feel very sorry for your mother. It's obvious she's getting sicker and sicker. Didn't you tell me once that she tastes and smells strange things whenever she's about to have a psychotic episode?"

Dorothy leaned against him feeling temporary safety in his embrace. The creak of the porch swing was reassuring. But all was not well.

"Malcolm," she asked. "Did you put sugar in my mother's tea?"

"Certainly not," he snapped. "You're beginning to sound just like her!"

Hurt, she pulled away from him. "I am not like her! But I did taste that tea, and it was sweetened."

"Well, if it was, Mrs. Crouch must have done it. She was acting just as batty as your mother tonight."

"But Malcolm, you told my mother that you made the tea. 'I poured it up myself,' you said."

"Look, Honey, don't you remember how you told me your mother hurt you so badly when you were just a little girl? I didn't want her to do that again. Mrs. Crouch handed me the tea but I told your mother I poured it myself just to shut her up and put an end to her little act."

"But didn't you taste the sugar when you sipped it?"

"It probably was still at the bottom of the cup. It must have gotten stirred up by the time we all passed it around. To tell you the truth, my taste buds are not that good. I just wanted to stop your mother's foolishness so you wouldn't be hurt."

"But why would Mrs. Crouch want to put sugar in the tea?"

"As I told you, she was as nutty as a fruitcake tonight."

Dorothy remembered the note. "Do you think Mrs. Crouch is nutty enough to write this?" Dorothy asked, pulling out the crayoned note.

For a moment, Malcolm was visibly shocked. The little pulse on his temple began to throb. Then he relaxed.

"It's just another of your mother's tricks, Honey. She's slipping, and soon you are going to have to make a decision to get her more help."

Even when Dorothy told Malcolm that Mrs. Crouch had been prowling around her room, Malcolm seemed to feel that Alicia, not the housekeeper, was responsible for the warning note. "But I'll keep this as evidence," he said, folding it to put in his pocket.

"Another thing bothers me," Dorothy continued, "Mrs. Crouch seems to think that my mother's preoccupation with sugar in her tea was somehow related to Aunt Patty's death."

The pulse began to throb again in Malcolm's temple and in his neck. He seemed angry. "Mrs. Crouch should not have told you anything! After all, Alicia is your mother and you do have some respect for her."

"I still don't understand," Dorothy persisted, "My brothers wrote me, and you told me, too, I think, that Patty went into a coma and died a few hours later. I just assumed she'd had a stroke."

"Her coma was brought on by the combination of sleeping medicine and a powerful tranquilizer," Malcolm told her. "Either one by itself probably wouldn't have hurt her, but the combination was lethal. There were drugs in her tea that day."

Looking squarely into Malcolm's grim face, Dorothy dreaded what she knew she must hear next.

Aunt Patty murdered! Her mother was not a murderess. Malicious, yes; she was capricious, willful, suspicious, and irresponsible, but not a murderess.

"Although your mother was never charged, there was some feeling that she was responsible for Aunt Patty's death."

Chapter 9

AUNT PATTY, ALTHOUGH NEVER A NERVOUS PERSON, had been taking various sleeping powders since Uncle Arthur died. But the tranquilizer was one that Alicia took. Patty had never taken a tranquilizer before. Why would she choose to do so that day?

The detectives had thought that perhaps Patty was despondent and had wanted to end her own life; but no, her friends testified that Patty was adjusting well to her husband's death. Still, perhaps she had wanted to borrow some tranquilizers from Alicia and had not realized how they would interact with her sleeping medication. And why had the medication been in the tea? Mrs. Crouch had insisted that Patty had had difficulty swallowing capsules and perhaps that was why she had emptied the contents of several of her capsules into her tea. But Mrs. Crouch was not sure. She had not seen anything. Neither had Malcolm.

Alicia could not be questioned because she had become catatonic and rigid, unable to speak, as a result of Patty's loss of consciousness and subsequent death. And when her episode was over days later, she could remember nothing. Alicia and Dorothy's father were living at Fox Hollow at this time, having been invited by Patty to move in and keep her company after Arthur's death. Dorothy's father, however, had been away for the day when Patty fell ill.

The investigators had asked the obvious questions of Malcolm, who had been there earlier, and Mrs. Crouch, who was there when the tea was poured. Could a person as disturbed as Alicia have deliberately done harm to Patty? Their answers had been, in essence, "Yes, Alicia could have done it. Yes, Alicia did have a mental illness. She sometimes did things she could not remember. But probably she had meant no harm, if, indeed, she had put something in the tea." Aunt Patty was one of the few persons who could get along with Alicia. Mrs. Crouch was careful to stress at the coroner's inquest that there had been no arguments between the women. They had been on friendly terms. Malcolm had not been able to add any useful information at the inquest. He had only been visiting Patty for a few days, and at that time, did not know Alicia very well.

Because there was no apparent motive for malicious intent, the investigation was not continued. Two women, one possibly despondent over her husband's death, and one an obvious mental case, had somehow combined their prescriptions to make a lethal dose for one of them. It was probably a tragic accident.

"But I suppose that Mrs. Crouch really thinks that your mother was somehow to blame," Malcolm continued, "and that's why she acts peculiar."

Any feeling of security Dorothy might have felt in Malcolm was gone. Her head was throbbing painfully. "I can't stand all this," she burst out, close to tears. "I simply cannot put up with this family any longer. I'm going back to Arizona!"

Jumping up, she whirled to go in, only to have Malcolm grab her arm and turn her back to face him.

"You are _not_ going back to Arizona. You are going to stay here and look after your mother as your father intended," he said evenly, holding her gaze.

The heavy perfume of wisteria and magnolia which had so consoled her now closed in to smother her. It's like a funeral, she thought. The humidity clung to her hair and her clothes and weighted her down. She longed suddenly for the clear dry air of the desert, with only cactus, which was not in bloom. The tears came.

"I don't know what to do. I called my firm today, and they cannot transfer me here. They asked me just to use my three weeks' leave and then reconsider. They will hold off my resignation until I'm sure."

Malcolm did not release her. "Good accountants are always in demand. I'll take you into Baton Rouge tomorrow. You can look for a job and an apartment, too."

"I just don't know what to do. I don't feel like choosing an apartment until I know if I'll get a job here."

"I have a better idea," said Malcolm. "We'll go into town but not just for a job or an apartment. Tomorrow we'll get our marriage license."

Chapter 10

STRETCHING HER LEGS LUXURIOUSLY, DOROTHY LOOKED AT the rose-patterned wallpaper in Aunt Patty's old sewing room. For a moment, she was a young girl again. The birds could be heard singing through the open window as the early morning sunlight made patterns in the room. But now the wallpaper was faded and beginning to be frayed along the top edges. On the ceiling were water stains. Dorothy was no longer a child. Remembering that decisions were to be made today, she felt the feeling of peace with which she awakened begin to evaporate.

But perhaps childish memories were what she needed. Children were often more in touch with reality than were adults, Dorothy thought. Suddenly she longed for Stephanie. She would spend the day with her child, away from the troubles of this house. Decisions about a job, an apartment, and even a marriage license could be postponed for one more day until she regained her sense of equilibrium.

Feeling strengthened by her decision to take a day off from family problems, she offered to carry up her mother's breakfast tray. Mrs. Crouch was busy cleaning and seemed glad to be relieved of the chore of waiting on Alicia. Dorothy was oddly relieved that Malcolm was still sleeping. She did not feel up to an argument about the marriage license.

Back in Arizona, she would have gone for the license as soon as Malcolm said the word, but he had always managed to talk around the issue. He had never asked her directly to marry him. Dorothy knew that he felt she should visit her father and try to resolve her family responsibilities first. Now that he was wiling to stand by her and help her, why was she dragging her feet? Perhaps she was still emotionally drained from the funeral; she felt it was too soon to rush into marriage.

Dorothy tapped lightly on her mother's door before trying the doorknob. She would tell her mother that she was going off today and perhaps she might not stay at Fox Hollow more than a few days longer. No doubt Alicia would be relieved to get Dorothy out of her hair. Dorothy could get some man at the bank to dole out Alicia's money and manage her expenses. Everything would probably turn out all right, and she and Malcolm and Stephanie could live happily ever after in Arizona. Even as she thought this, however, her guilty conscience gave way to visions of her mother being swindled out of her money, or worse yet, her mother becoming more mentally ill and hurting herself or someone else.

The door was opened warily by a haggard Alicia. Her blonde hair was frizzy and uncombed, and under her eyes were dark circles. For once in her life, she did not look much younger than her years. "I haven't slept a wink," she said.

Setting the tray down on her mother's mahogany bedside table, Dorothy queried, "What on earth is wrong?"

Alicia took an inordinately long time to adjust her satin quilted robe, arrange her tray on the edge of the bed, and settle herself back into the bed under the comforter. Frequently, Alicia enjoyed being melodramatic but today, however, Dorothy felt that Alicia was not just acting.

"I was watching television-you know the best actress awards," she began. "Now what is that actress's name-you know, the one who played…"

"Tell me what happened to upset you," Dorothy interrupted. She did not want to hear about the television awards.

"That's what I was doing before you rudely interrupted me," Alicia snapped peevishly. "Now I've lost my train of thought. Now let's see-where was I? They gave the award to that actress I don't care for."

"Is that what upset you?" Dorothy asked.

"I'm trying to tell you if you'll stop being so rude and let me."

Dorothy sighed and settled herself as best she could into a rose velvet Victorian loveseat. She knew she would have to hear about all the TV personalities before her mother would get to the point. She let her gaze wander about the room. Her mother loved the Victorian period best although the home was furnished, like most people's homes, in a conglomeration of periods. In several glass cases were collections belonging to her mother. Dorothy could never decide which were her favorites, the birds or the bells. Her mother had most of the bird figurines issued: the robin, the bluebird, the cardinal. Their love of birds was one of the few interests Alicia and Dorothy had in common. Once when she was not much older than Stephanie, her mother had made her a bird feeder from an old can and pie plate-the kind that had peanut butter inside. They had hung it on the magnolia limb outside the dining room window. How thrilled Dorothy had been when some birds actually came to eat! For several birthdays and Mothers' Days which followed, she and her father had bought bird figurines for Alicia.

Most of the bells, on the other hand, had been bought by Alicia for herself whenever she visited a new place of interest. There were pewter bells, silver bells, brass bells, crystal bells, and china bells. One was made to look like a lady's skirt. Others had dates and the names of places inscribed. Dorothy had loved to ring the bells when she was a child-until she broke one. "I treasured that one most of all," her mother had said, "and you re to blame that it can never be replaced. It is your fault that I have problems with my nerves."

Many things can never be replaced, thought Dorothy the adult, like the affections of childhood. The total impression one might get from Alicia's room was, Dorothy decided: here is a woman who loves beauty, but the furniture is not comfortable and the bric-a-brac is not to be touched. Dorothy was reminded of a new folk song, the one about the lemon tree with pretty flowers but with fruit that was impossible to eat.

Dorothy, you are not listening," Alicia's voice brought her back. She had risen from her bed and walked to the old-fashioned bureau with tiny brass locks on each drawer. "I fell asleep during the awards because I took a new sleeping pill-not the one given by my old doctor but the one I got when I went to see that new man. Did I tell you his name?"

"No," said Dorothy, settling herself down again in preparation for another verbal barrage. Suddenly her mother said in a plaintive voice, "Please don't go back to Arizona just yet! I have no one I can trust but you. Someone wants to hurt me!"

Turning around, Alicia held a note in her hand which read, "You will be punished for every wicked thing you have done. In your heart you know you are a bad person."

The note was crudely crayoned on lined notebook paper. Every letter was a different color!

Chapter 11

With a sense of relief, Dorothy drove toward her brother Phillip's house. It was already late morning. It had taken some time to calm Alicia down after she revealed to Dorothy the note she had received. Dorothy now was convinced that Mrs. Crouch must be the culprit, not her mother. She even felt a pang of guilt that she had suspected her mother so quickly, whereas her mother had not accused her of doing the same. Alicia's agitation had not been feigned. Yet when Dorothy had gently tried to get her mother to admit what Mrs. Crouch had against her, Alicia had been unwilling to discuss the housekeeper.

"Why do you keep her when she's so disagreeable?" Dorothy had persisted, "You don't keep her for her cooking, I'm sure." Her mother's eggs, now cold, appeared to look up at them reproachfully, like two congealed yellow eyes.

"Oh, because your father liked her. That's why," Alicia answered vaguely, dismissing the topic. "It must have been that little snip, Harriet, who did this." Alicia continued. "I told Scott he shouldn't have married her, and look what she's done. Isn't that just like a bar maid?" she added self-righteously. "Why do you suppose Scott wanted to marry a bar maid who would threaten his mother?"

Harriet was another possibility, Dorothy admitted. Yet Dorothy could not imagine the red-haired girl in this role. Harriet had seemed more hurt than vengeful.

After Dorothy told Alicia she was going to take Stephanie on an outing, Alicia had wanted to come. "I don't know why I can't see my own grandchild," she said. "Just because she's illegitimate doesn't mean she's not my grandchild, does it?"

Then, looking at Dorothy with pity, she had said, "But of course you're too ashamed. Well, you aren't the only person in the world with a bastard child. Carlotta has one too, you know. Isn't that the limit? I have only two grandchildren and both of them are born out of season. Only, I guess Carlotta's baby is not a real grandchild. If Phillip isn't the father, then it isn't my grandchild. Isn't that right? But it doesn't matter who you slept with-your baby is still my grandchild because it's yours. Why couldn't all of you have behaved yourselves so I could have the right kind of grandchildren like I'm supposed to? Young people are so inconsiderate."

In a heroic effort to keep her temper, Dorothy had said nothing. But what was her mother babbling about Carlotta? She had already heard that Carlotta was pregnant when she and Phillip married; but that didn't mean that the baby, Sara, was not his daughter. It was obvious to Dorothy that Phillip was very attached to the child. Her mother's mind was playing malicious tricks again, Dorothy concluded.

"I am tired of your making up vicious stories about everyone," Dorothy had lashed out at Alicia. "If you can't use your imagination for something constructive, you should just keep quiet!" Leaving the distraught and startled Alicia finally speechless, Dorothy had stormed out of her mother's room and out of the house, which now seemed to harbor such ill will toward all its inhabitants.

As she rounded the curve in the driveway and saw the barbed wire fence bordering the pasture, where Uncle Arthur's horses were once kept, Dorothy saw the faded black and white sign "Fox Hollow" at the entrance. She remembered the connection between the name of Fox Hollow and the horses. Before Uncle Arthur had bought Fox Hollow, the land had been used as part of a hunting club. The members of this club had actually dressed in red coats and riding breeches and had straddled fine horses on English saddles as they pursued the fox. Uncle Arthur, who loved horses, had ridden in the hunt a few times. But, as he later told Dorothy, he had lost interest in the sport when he came upon the fox, which was surrounded by hounds. Usually the fox got away, or if it was killed, it happened somewhere out of sight. But this time he had come in time to see the kill and had felt sympathy and reverent admiration for the animal's valiant fight. Even though blood soaked the animal's fur, it had maintained a certain dignity, as it turned, back arched almost like a cat, to face the hounds for the last time. Uncle Arthur continued to ride his horses, but he lost his taste for cornering a fox.

Once Uncle Arthur, in an effort to help Dorothy understand her mother's irrational temper fits, had said, "Some people are like the fox in the hunt. Life's ordinary pressures are, to them, persecutions. They feel hounded until they are forced to turn and lash out at their perceived attackers." Dorothy had not been convinced. Her mother, in her opinion, was more like a pampered house pet who bit or scratched the hands that fed it. She was more like a sleek, well-cared-for tabby than like a fox pursued by hounds. But somebody really was pursuing Alicia now, as well as Dorothy. Who could be behind those childish, spiteful notes?

When eventually the hunt club was disbanded, Uncle Arthur had been able to buy 10 acres of what was considered the less desirable section because part of it was swampy. The house, which was close to the bayou and swamp, had been built in 1906 by one of the founders of the club. Dorothy had seen the year 1906 on a cement block at the corner of the house.

When Uncle Arthur and Aunt Patty had moved in, they renovated the bathrooms and kitchen, added a modern heating system, refinished the floors, and of course, painted and added the wallpaper in the bedrooms. Some of those things needed to be done again, Dorothy realized, if only Alicia would allow it. Renovations, with their attendant noise and dirt, made Alicia nervous.

Driving across the green countryside partially restored Dorothy's spirits. She would take Stephanie to the shopping mall and buy her the shoes she needed. They would get a red balloon. And perhaps they would eat lunch at the little sidewalk café which served twenty-seven flavors of ice cream.

She was sure her mother was wrong about Phillip's and Carlotta's baby. Why must Alicia always imagine the worst about people? Still, Dorothy wished she could like Carlotta better.

To her dismay, Dorothy found Carlotta dressed and waiting for her. "I'm taking you to lunch," she said, flashing a smile. "We don't even have to take the kids. We can leave them here with Mattie and have ourselves a shopping spree."

This was not the day that Dorothy had planned. She had wanted to be alone with Stephanie. But how could she tell Carlotta not to come, especially since Carlotta was trying to be nice?

"I really do have to get Stephanie shoes," she said, "but we can still have lunch."

"I always just guess what size Sara wears," Carlotta said with a shrug, "I never take her anywhere because I can't stand it when little kids act up in public. But suit yourself."

As it turned out, Carlotta and Stephanie both accompanied Dorothy to the shopping mall, but they parted for shopping. While Dorothy bought Stephanie shoes and explored several toy departments, Carlotta pursued her own interests. Later, the three met at the sidewalk café. Stephanie, wearing new shoes and clutching a red balloon, fortunately behaved herself. She was eating a peanut butter sandwich and a clown ice cream cone.

Dorothy sensed that Carlotta wanted to share something. Lighting a cigarette, the dark-haired woman leaned toward Dorothy in a confidential manner. "Tell me," she said slyly, her dark eyes gleaming with curiosity, "what do you do to keep Malcolm interested in you?"

Dorothy blushed. "I don't know what you mean." Was their physical attraction to each other so obvious?

"Oh come on," continued Carlotta. "He's obviously crazy about you. Are you getting married soon?"

Dorothy had started to say "yes" but held herself in check. She wondered why this woman needed to know.

"Where did you hear that?" she asked, putting her sister-in-law off.

"Well," said Carlotta, feeling rebuffed, "I just wanted to learn your secrets. I can't keep Phillip interested in me. He's having an affair!"

Dorothy's head was reeling. Her mother had made up a wild story about Carlotta cheating on Phillip, but now Carlotta claimed that Phillip was unfaithful!

So intent was Dorothy on Carlotta's revelation that she failed to notice when Stephanie slipped away from the table. Rising abruptly, Dorothy now rushed into the open mall area. The red balloon made it easy to spot Stephanie. She had not gone far-just to the pet store window across the way. But already Stephanie was talking to an older woman, probably some nice motherly type who was concerned that the child was lost.

Suddenly Dorothy froze in her tracks. Her partially-eaten lunch lurched disturbingly in her middle. The woman Stephanie was talking to was Dorothy's former mother-in law!

Chapter 12

Moving behind a concrete planter in the center of the open mall, Dorothy pondered what to do. Stephen's mother was the last person she wanted to see. Perhaps she would go away soon and Dorothy could retrieve her daughter. Dorothy was aware that Stephanie looked like Stephen's side of the family, but surely this woman would not notice. She did not know she had a granddaughter, and even if she had heard, she would surely not be able to spot her grandchild in a crowd. Peering from behind a palm frond, Dorothy listened.

"What's your name, dear?" the older woman asked.

For once Dorothy wished her child were not so outgoing.

"Stephanie Michelle," the little girl lisped.

The older woman looked thoughtful. Her son's name was Stephen Michael. Would she make the connection? Dorothy, in a moment of weakness, had named the child after her father. Realizing that she could not give the child her father's last name, she had thought she could at least bestow his first and middle name on the baby. Now, she wished she had called the child "Jane," or "Myrtle" –anything but Stephanie Michelle.

Dorothy had an inspiration. She would hurry back and get Carlotta. Let Carlotta pretend to be the mother. Then Mrs. Smith would lose interest in Stephanie and go away. Standing shielded behind the plants, Dorothy sidled back to the café table, where she quickly enlisted Carlotta's help.

"It's Stephen's mother," she whispered frantically. "I don't want her to know I have a child by her son. You go get Stephanie and I will stay hidden." Carlotta scurried off and Dorothy stayed out of sight, waiting nervously. She paid her bill at the cash register and looked surreptitiously in the direction of the mall. Moments passed but they did not return. Cautiously, Dorothy edged back into the mall area toward the planter again. Once more she peeked from behind palm fronds and saw Carlotta and the older woman carrying on an animated conversation. Whatever had they found to chatter about? Stephanie looked bored and poised for flight again. Finally, Mrs. Smith turned and walked in the opposite direction. After a safe period of time, Dorothy emerged.

"What did she say," Dorothy asked Carlotta. "You didn't let her know I was here?"

"Oh heavens no, we didn't discuss who I was, much less who the kid was. She just wanted to tell me about the good old days when she was little. Old people do like to run off at the mouth."

Dorothy heaved a sigh of relief. She had momentarily escaped an unpleasant confrontation. She should have known it was a mistake to bring Stephanie back to this part of the country-near her father and grandmother Smith.

On the way home, Carlotta told Dorothy more about Phillip and his infatuation for a girl in the store where he worked. Dorothy remembered another young man who was supposed to be infatuated with a girl at work: Stephen. "Maybe it's just a business friendship," she suggested. "I wouldn't worry."

Carlotta gave her a withering look. "Honey, Phillip doesn't have but one kind of relationship."

Even if this were true, Dorothy did not like to hear such talk about her brother. She was relieved to deliver Carlotta to her door. She did not really want to give Stephanie back to Mattie, but for the time being, it was the wisest plan. She did not want the child at Fox Hollow where malice seemed to be brewing. Perhaps in a day or two she would get a place of her own-or else make a decision to return to Arizona.

Suddenly Dorothy decided to look at apartment complexes. Perhaps looking at potential home sites would help her decide. Could she and Stephanie be as happy here as they had been in Arizona?

Chapter 13

Dorothy had met Stephen in a math class in college. He was in engineering; she was studying accounting. Both were enrolled in calculus.

For several years, Dorothy had run her parents' household. Alicia had been hospitalized for her longest period during Dorothy's teens. It was felt that she might never recover, so from the age of fourteen to almost seventeen, Dorothy had assumed the homemaker's role. In a way, it had been easier with her mother gone. Dorothy could be completely in charge.

The first time Dorothy had had to take charge was when she was about eight. Evidently, the mother had not been bothered with mental health symptoms when Dorothy was very young. At least she had had mostly happy memories of the family when she was very young. But when Phillip was born and Scott two years later, Alicia's mental health deteriorated. Dorothy was in second grade when she realized that something was very wrong in her family's household. For one thing, her mother was always sleeping. The pills she took for her nerves made her extremely groggy. Her father had grown worried and grim. Once a dark-headed and dashingly handsome man, he now had permanent creases in his forehead and seemed to be perpetually frowning. His hair turned prematurely grey.

Because Alicia became increasingly helpless, the family had hired a series of maids. None could get along with Alicia more than a few weeks. None except Jessie. Jessie had been a tall, skinny, mulatto woman with a lot of spirit as well as compassion. Full of spunk, she had known when to stand up to Alicia and when to shrug off her insults. Jessie had looked after the two baby boys, had kept the house spotless, done the laundry, and cooked special treats for Dorothy.

But even Jessie could not last forever in the Deveroux household. Alicia must have taken off her diamond wedding rings when she washed her hands, Somehow the rings had been mislaid. Alicia, however, was convinced that Jessie had stolen the rings. The scenes which followed were painful to remember. First, there was a hysterical scene with Dorothy's father. Alicia had cried and carried on until he agreed to fire Jessie. Then came the confrontation with the maid. This gaunt, energetic woman, who had come into the household full of pride, was now humiliated and stripped of her dignity. Dorothy stood sadly in the doorway, watching as Jessie left. On that particular day, Jessie, not knowing what lay in store for her, had brought a present of candy for Dorothy. Now, as she was leaving, she turned and handed Dorothy a rumpled paper bag. "Here's those chocolates I promised you," her gold teeth glistening against her dark, yellow-skinned face. "You're a nice girl, Dorothy. It's a pity you are white."

"Why?" Dorothy had asked. "What does it matter if I'm white?"

"Because you'll grow up evil," Jessie answered. "Like her."

Later, when Dorothy had found her mother's rings on the carpet, she had wanted to call Jessie. But her mother would not allow it.

The departure of Jessie meant more work for Dorothy. Her father was at his wits' end. "I have to leave for my office downtown at seven," he told Dorothy. "If you don't take care of your brothers, I can't work. I have to depend on you."

Dorothy did not want her father to lose his job. She would have to give up her room. She had visions of the family moving into the street, carrying little bundles. It might be fun to camp in the park, she thought, but it would not be fun to have no food or toys or clothes. No, this must not happen. So early every morning, Dorothy slipped out of bed to take care of her brothers. If they cried, her mother would not hear. If it were not for her, Dorothy knew the babies might even die.

She always fixed cereal and bananas for Phillip at his little table. Then she lifted Scott out of his crib, changed him, and put him in his high chair. For him, she prepared a bottle and cooked some baby cereal, which she shoveled into his mouth with a little spoon. Sometimes she gave him a jar of baby fruit, too. Next, she put Scott back in his crib with a bottle while she got Phillip dressed. She then bathed Scott and put fresh baby clothes on him. Dorothy rode a school bus that year, which luckily, did not come until half past eight. By that time, she barely had time to slip into her own clothes and leave for school. She was now in third grade.

Sometimes Alicia was able to struggle awake before Dorothy left for school. If not, Dorothy would call an elderly neighbor who would come and sit until Alicia woke up. Dorothy never left until the baby was safe in a crib or pen and Phillip was parked in front of his favorite TV cartoons. She knew her father would come home for lunch, and that after lunch, the boys could be put down for naps. By this time Alicia was usually awake. Still, she felt obligated to hurry home after school to be sure everything was all right.

Gradually Alicia seemed to cope better, although several brief hospital stays were necessary during Dorothy's childhood. On several occasions, Aunt Patty came. At other times, Alicia seemed normal, and the Deveroux family lived like any other family. Yet Dorothy was constantly alert for signs. She seemed to have developed an antenna attuned to her mother's moods. She knew she must never take normalcy and happiness for granted.

During the teen years while Alicia was gone, Dorothy's adjustment was fairly easy. While at one level she was sad about her mother's illness, especially since her father took it so hard, at another level she was relieved not to have to second guess her mother's moods on a daily basis. Before, she had had to ask herself each day as she returned from school, "Will she be all right today?" Now that the worst had happened, it was a relief. Her mother was not all right. Her mother was in a mental hospital. But it was out of Dorothy's hands. And that was a relief.

Although Dorothy became less anxious and tense, she was still not a sociable teenager. There were always chores to do at night. And, except for her brief summer romance with her cousin Malcolm, there had been no serious boyfriends until Stephen.

The hardest year of Dorothy's life was the year her mother was finally released from the hospital. Perhaps Alicia felt guilty that Dorothy had been burdened with so many chores and wanted to take some of the load off her daughter. Or, more likely, Alicia wanted to prove that she was an able, competent homemaker and was jealous that Dorothy had usurped her position as rightful head of the household. Suddenly Dorothy, who had been accustomed to cooking all the family meals, was considered too stupid to set the table, not bright enough to make a salad. When Dorothy tried to help, her mother gave orders and criticized her every move. But if Dorothy refused to help, her mother called her lazy. Anger was Dorothy's constant companion, but she dared not express this anger lest her mother become ill again.

It particularly hurt Dorothy to see the discipline of her younger brothers undermined. They were accustomed to minding Dorothy. Now she would tell them to do one thing and then her mother would tell them to do the opposite. Later, Dorothy wondered if this lack of consistency had led to the development of their weak characters.

Although Dorothy was constantly angry, she felt like her mother was like a fine china vase which had been shattered and then glued back together. Any little trauma might shatter this vase once more, and she did not want to be the one guilty of sending her mother back to the hospital. As soon as she graduated from high school, she escaped to the campus of one of the state colleges.

Chapter 14

MATH WAS DOROTHY'S BEST SUBJECT. SHE DID not care much for political science or literature, where ambiguities in interpretation were possible. In math, everything was concrete; an equation was either right or wrong. And theorems held true in every case. She had seen enough of relativity. Fantasy and creative interpretations of events were threatening to her rather than stimulating, in her opinion. Had she not lived in the house with a divergent thinker who had placed her own subjective interpretations on every daily event? Divergence reminded Dorothy of Alicia. She preferred concrete reality and objectivity.

Stephen had his own quirk of personality in that he had difficulty expressing his emotions. When his father had left the family after his sister had died, his mother had tried to maintain too strong of a relationship with him. He was all she had. Stephen's defensive reaction had been to insulate himself from any emotional display. Tall, blonde, and thin, he was intense about his work. His other feelings were tightly controlled, all of which suited Dorothy fine. Remembering Alicia's emotional excesses, her habit of exploiting the feelings of others, made Dorothy feel more comfortable around people who did not show too much emotion. Yet the feelings Dorothy and Stephen had for each other had been intense, at least while the relationship lasted.

Their courtship had actually lasted longer than their marriage. Because both were socially shy and diffident, their friendship took several years to develop to the point where marriage was considered.

By going to summer school each year, Dorothy had managed to get a Masters' degree in accounting in four years. She had no trouble finding a job. Although Stephen was not yet through his engineering courses- he had chosen a more difficult project than the average engineering student-they married and moved to a small apartment near campus.

Stephen's mother had wanted him to finish his degree before marriage, but after she saw Dorothy had a good job, she gave her grudging approval. She did not appear to be as possessive and domineering as Stephen had described her. She was not warm toward Dorothy, but was reasonably pleasant. Dorothy's parents, on the other hand, had hoped she would move back home and help them run the household. Even though one brother was ready for college and the other was in high school, and even though Alicia's mental health was better, the family still had trouble with the daily tasks of living. The responsibilities of laundry and cooking were too much for Alicia to do alone, yet she resented any help given by other family members because such help was a reminder of her own incompetence. In addition, Phillip and Scott were unwilling to do much work around the home, and they had caused the parents some grief with their teen-aged antics.

In the end, Alicia, perhaps fearing that Dorothy would take over her place in the home again, had advised her to go ahead and marry Stephen.

"He seems kind of dull," Alicia had said, "but then you might not get another offer. You are too aggressive and strong and that scares men off. If you would be more feminine like me, you would have more offers."

The next few months were Dorothy's happiest. To outsiders, she and Stephen might seem like a dull couple; to each other they were far from dull. They were totally happy. But this idyllic state could not last. When they had been married for less than a year, Dorothy's mother came to visit.

Alicia seemed to be making a sincere effort to be nice and become closer to her daughter. She bought presents for Dorothy and Stephen and treated them to dinner in a restaurant they could not have afforded on Dorothy's salary. Gradually, Dorothy began to relax and accept her mother. If Alicia had really changed, Dorothy could overlook the problems they had had in the past. After all, Alicia had been mentally ill. She probably didn't mean all the things she had said to hurt Dorothy over the years. Or, if she did mean to say them, she probably couldn't help it. Perhaps her illness was finally cured and they could be friends.

But even when Alicia was trying to be pleasant, her emotional displays created tension in the little apartment. Dorothy could not forget the image of her mother as a piece of china that had been glued together. Might she not suddenly shatter again? Stephen, not normally gregarious anyway, found reasons to escape Alicia's and Dorothy's feminine conversations. He said he had to work overtime on his engineering project. Dorothy's mother did not believe it.

"If I were you, I would find out where he really goes every night," she advised Dorothy. "You can't trust a man."

"I don't know what you mean," Dorothy had answered defensively.

"He said he had to study, but I happen to know that the library is closed tonight. I saw the hours for the library on some paper he brought home," she added, proud of her snooping.

"He doesn't go to the main library," Dorothy had countered. "He goes to some room in the engineering building. Actually, he's building some kind of model."

"I see," Alicia had said with meaning. Dorothy knew that her mother still did not believe Stephen was really working.

The following evening, after Dorothy had come in from work and Stephen had left again, Dorothy's mother could hardly wait to break her news.

"I shouldn't think he would need to run off again," she said. "He's already seen her once today."

"Seen who?" Dorothy had wanted to know.

"The girl. The one he's cheating with. She had the audacity to come to the apartment today after you had gone to work. That's what you get for going to work to support a man. I told you he wouldn't appreciate it; in my day the man did the supporting..." Alicia seemed poised to launch into a lecture about the proper roles for males and females. In her view, the traditional roles were the only proper ones. Dorothy was determined to get her mother back on the subject.

"If you don't come to the point, I'll scream! Who was the girl who came to the apartment?"

"Well" said Alicia, taking time to sip from a cup of tea and wiped her mouth daintily, "he said..." (Here again, Alicia emphasized the word "said.".) "He said she was an engineering student and she was going to help him with his project."

"Well then, I'm sure she was," Dorothy snapped. Yet she wondered, why did the girl come to the apartment? The project was in the engineering building. And why hadn't Stephen mentioned her?

"Oh Dorothy, for a smart girl you are so dense. You'd believe anything anyone told you. Engineering students don't look like that."

Dorothy's mother went on to relate how the girl had looked: honey blonde hair and dimples. A heart-shaped face and blue eyes. And, of course, she was petite and dainty, not tall and large-boned like Dorothy.

"If I were you, I'd confront him with it," Alicia had advised. "Demand that he not see her again, no matter what his excuse. You have to stop them when they first start chasing. If he gets away with this, he'll just do it again."

Although Dorothy had told Alicia to stop imagining things, she was troubled. Could she hope to compete with a honey blonde, dimpled and dainty engineering student?

The following evening Dorothy's mother volunteered to buy them dinner. Stephen begged off. "I'm almost finished with my project," he said. "It's at a critical stage."

Dorothy had wanted to ask whether or not the blonde was going to help and if so, was she at a critical stage, but she held her tongue. Her mother was listening and seemed to be savoring the possibility of a row. Her face had the look of a cat ready to pounce on an unsuspecting bird. How Alicia would love to see some sparks fly between the normally placid Dorothy and Stephen. No, Dorothy decided, she would discuss the blonde with Stephen later, after Alicia had gone home. Alicia had a reservation tonight at ten on the shuttle plane to take her home. She would take Alicia to dinner and then to her plane. The blonde could wait.

Instead of a fancy restaurant, Alicia chose a spaghetti house. Dorothy wondered at her selection because it would have been simple to fix spaghetti at home. Alicia, to her knowledge, was never crazy about Italian food.

Before the hostess could seat them, Dorothy saw him. Sitting at a corner table sat Stephen with the blonde. In the candlelight, which flickered from an old wine bottle, Stephen's intelligent expression seemed focused on whatever the girl was saying. She was the most beautiful girl Dorothy had ever seen.

Dorothy would have liked to have backed up and slipped quickly out the front door from which they had entered before Stephen and his companion looked up. But Alicia, already ahead of Dorothy, would not have it so. Brazenly, she strode to their table and said in a loud voice, "Well, Stephen, I thought you were working. Look Dorothy, see who is here!"

The scene which followed was embarrassing to all concerned, except perhaps to Alicia, who thrived on such fare. Her eyes, in fact, fairly glittered with excitement to think she had been right in her suspicions. Stephen and the girl, whose name was Susan, made a feeble effort to seat Alicia and Dorothy, but Dorothy dragged Alicia away almost bodily and took her to a Chinese restaurant across the street. Once seated, she sat, miserable and embarrassed, unable to taste her soggy egg roll. She had the feeling nothing would ever be the same. Perhaps she was no longer herself. She must be living out a fantasy, as Alicia did at times. Perhaps she had become a character in a soap opera.

Alicia, by contrast, seemed in better mental health than Dorothy. She gobbled her chop suey with relish and chattered gaily. Generously, she offered to cancel her plane reservations to "be there" for Dorothy. "I can see you need me," she said.

When Dorothy made it clear she did not need Alicia to stay longer, Alicia made her promise to come visit soon-"without that dreadful skirt chaser." With some relief, Dorothy helped her mother to board the little plane which would take her 100 miles away. She did not see Alicia again for more than three years.

Chapter 15

Dorothy underestimated how angry Stephen would be. She had embarrassed him in front of his colleague. His interest in Susan, he maintained, was purely professional. Yes, she was an engineering student who had done work in the same area he was doing. With her help he would soon be able to solve the difficult problem which had been a stumbling block to his graduation.

Dorothy had assumed that she had more right to be angry than Stephen did. Had she not been deceived? She assumed wrong. Her lack of trust, Stephen felt, was more serious than his liason with an attractive student.

He had not intended to go with Susan to dinner, but when he had called her to meet him at the lab, she said she was getting a quick bite at the spaghetti house. He may as well join her and then they would go to the lab. Dorothy and her mother were planning to eat out anyway, probably at one of those fancy restaurants he didn't care for. Unfortunately, Alicia had been listening in to the telephone conversation. That explained her sudden interest in spaghetti.

As Stephen pointed out, Dorothy worked in an all-male office. Did he come to her work and make a scene? No, he trusted her. Without trust, a relationship could not survive.

Dorothy and Stephen did not make up either that day or the next. Both went to bed nursing their own set of grievances. In the morning she slipped out without waking him and went to work early.

It was Friday, Stephen's mother's birthday. They had planned to drive to his mother's home and spend the night. Stephen's mother lived somewhat near Aunt Patty's and Uncle Arthur's home, about 80 miles from the university campus.

Stephen and Dorothy's original plan had been to get off work and school early in order to leave by 4:30 p.m. They could arrive in time to have dinner with his mother. Dorothy did take the afternoon off from work. But she had another purpose. She had a doctor's appointment at two. Surely she would be home by four. As in most doctors' offices, however, a crowd of patients was waiting. Dorothy did not get home until after four thirty. Stephen had already left for his mother's house.

At first, Dorothy was angry. What would his mother think? He had left her for spite. Although Stephen had been slow to anger, he was also slow to get over his anger.

Rationally, Dorothy tried to understand. When she had not returned home by four thirty, he might have assumed that she was not coming. After all, she had left the house without speaking that morning. She knew Stephen was stubborn. She would have to take the initiative if they were going to make up. Because of what she had learned at the doctor's office, she was willing to make the effort. She would find a present for Stephen's mother and drive up to her home with it. Stephen would have to be nice to her if she arrived with a birthday gift for his mother. And when he heard that they were going to have a baby, he would forget his bad mood entirely.

Buoyed up by her determination to make things right, Dorothy quickly put her overnight bag in the car and stopped by a shopping center to select her mother-in-law's favorite scent. She would be a little late for dinner but they would be glad to see her. They would have to be!

Stephen's mother did not have as much land as Aunt Patty and Uncle Arthur had, but she had a large house. Her home was a more formal, colonial type, with white pillars. Stephen's car was in the circular drive, beside his mother's. At least they had not gone out to dinner. Although Dorothy rang the bell several times, nothing happened. If Stephen and his mother were in the dining room, they should be able to hear the chimes. It was already dark. No doubt dinner was over and Stephen and his mother were on the brick patio behind the house. Because the front door was locked, Dorothy decided to walk around to the rear of the house. As she had thought, they were sitting on the patio. She could see their shapes outlined in the near dark. Honeysuckle and gardenia gave the air a heavy, sweet scent. Because of the shrubbery and the way their chairs were facing, they could not see her coming. She was just about to call out when she heard her name spoken. Years later, she realized she should not have listened. If she had made her presence known, much pain could have been avoided.

"It's a pity Dorothy couldn't come," Mrs. Smith was saying.

"She's been upset and mad the past few days," Stephen replied. "Her mother got her suspicious and stirred up about something."

Dorothy began to bristle. How dare he discuss their affairs so casually?

"What on earth is the matter with that Mrs. Deveroux?" Mrs. Smith asked.

"She definitely has schizophrenia. The doctors disagree on whether or not it's the paranoid type, but she does have some type of schizophrenia. They seem to agree on that."

"Well, if she's suspicious, she must be paranoid," Mrs. Smith commented.

"I don't care what you call it. The woman definitely has a talent for thinking the worst about people. She attributes only the very meanest of motives to others."

In the darkness Dorothy shivered. What they said about her mother was true, but she did not like to hear her family discussed in such clinical terms. But the worst was yet to come. A mosquito bit her, yet she did not move to scratch.

"I don't think you and Dorothy should have children," Mrs. Smith said. "Dorothy seems to be a sweet girl, but so was her mother at one time, I've heard."

Stephen protested, "I know she will never get like her mother."

"It doesn't show up until later sometimes," Mrs. Smith warned, "And even if Dorothy doesn't become mentally ill herself, she will pass it to any children you and she might have. That type of illness is terribly hereditary, you know."

"Don't worry, we're not having any kids for a long time. I don't even have a job."

"What I'm saying, Stephen, is that you must never have any children!"

Shame is not the same as guilt, Dorothy had once read in psychology class 101. Guilt was the result of a wrong act which one had committed. Shame, on the other hand, was when one suffered deep humiliation because of a condition over which one had no control. Guilt, although the result of a deliberate wrong act, was the more productive of the two emotions. Unlike shame, guilt offered the promise of hope. By refusing to sin again or by making amends for one's past deeds, one could hope to win relief from guilt. But shame was a state from which there was no escape. It resulted from what one was, not what one did. An example might be a person with a physical deformity. Even though the person had done nothing to deserve the handicap, the person might still be subjected to taunts or mistreatment. Perhaps some black people felt this way before they developed racial pride. The humiliation of who one was could not be mitigated by any number of good deeds.

In the dark, Dorothy could feel herself flush. Shame threatened to crush her and grind her and push her into the ground. She was amazed to realize that she was still standing. It had never occurred to her that she would be judged for something beyond her control, her mother's illness!

As a child, Dorothy had always believed that if she were responsible and hard-working, she could make herself as good as other people. If anything, people seemed to think highly of her because she took care of her little brothers, worked hard in the home, and still did well in school. It had never occurred to her that she had to be a helpless pawn in life. But now she realized that because of her family's medical history, she could never hope to be considered a worthwhile person.

Stepping back softly, she faded into the blackness of the night. Turning, she fairly ran to the car. For some odd reason, she stopped and put her mother-in-law's present on the front step. Then she returned to the car and drove away. In a relatively short time, she was turning into Aunt Patty's and Uncle Arthur's driveway. They had been her refuge in childhood. They would help her now.

Unfortunately, Aunt Patty and Uncle Arthur were not home. Even the door to the screened section of the porch was locked. Curling up on the chaise lounge on the open part of the veranda, she decided to wait for them. By this time, a thunder storm was imminent.

Although sheltered by the overhanging eaves, Dorothy was sprayed by the wind-blown rain. The lightning, crashing all around her, was no less tumultuous than her state of mind. Lack of food made her nauseated and the dampness made her cold, but her physical discomfort was secondary to her mental pain. Stephen did not want a child now and his mother did not want one ever. She began to shiver. Maybe she would lose her baby. It would be better if she did. It would save her the trouble of having to destroy it.

Aunt Patty and Uncle Arthur still had not come when the sun's first rays cast their glow over the rain-drenched landscape. No doubt they had gone somewhere for the weekend. All around her, birds twittered, singing their hearts out. It was a new day. Thoroughly numb and stiff, Dorothy roused herself from where she had huddled in a miserable heap and made her way to the steps. A water moccasin had slithered from the lower ground near the rain-swollen bayou and lay poised to strike. It seemed to stare at her, its white mouth open. She stared back, unafraid, and walked around it.

Once inside the car, warmed by its heater, Dorothy's fighting spirit returned. She and her baby had survived the night. They would continue to survive.

Chapter 16

DRIVING HOME IN THE EARLY MORNING LIGHT, Dorothy felt a surge of love for her unborn child. It was going to be strong like she was. She had not miscarried. She would not get rid of this pregnancy. To do so would be to admit defeat. Her mother-in-law had implied that she was not good enough to have a baby. She would prove Mrs. Smith wrong. She would not get mentally ill, and neither would her child.

In her mind flashed a picture of a mentally ill child she had once seen in the state hospital. While waiting in the depressing lobby of the hospital for her mother to come out, a nurse had led in a little girl about seven years old. A pretty dark-haired child, the little girl did not acknowledge any visitors. Instead, she had announced to the air, "I don't like dogs!" Then, whirling about and changing her voice, the child had answered herself, "But they won't hurt you." Quickly, the nurse hurried the child away. Would she produce a child like that poor girl? Dorothy wondered.

Realistically, Dorothy knew that Stephen's mother had a right to be concerned. Mental illness did seem to occur more frequently in some families. But, Dorothy wondered, could it be possible that in these families, children learned inappropriate behavior from watching their disturbed relatives? Or, in other cases, a child might be constantly reminded that "Uncle Charlie went crazy, so I hope you don't turn out like him." Such a child might then fulfill the prophecy.

She knew what she must do. Her baby must not ever see nor hear about Alicia. And if this meant leaving Stephen, she would do what she had to do.

She knew that Stephen would not be in the apartment so early in the morning. Probably he and his mother were just now having breakfast. She would have time to pack before he returned.

Passing her bureau mirror, she caught a glimpse of her reflection and was frightened by her wildness. Her hair was unkempt, her clothing wet and rumpled, her eyes too bright and feverish. If Stephen and his mother could see her now, their suspicions would be confirmed. "It's happening sooner than we thought," they would say. She took time to shower and wash her hair. Never must she give the impression that she was disoriented, not in control. Wearing clean clothes, with her hair smooth and make up on, Dorothy was once more in charge. The packing did not take long since theirs was a furnished apartment. He could have the few wedding gifts.

Writing the note was more difficult. Perhaps it would not be necessary. Maybe they could still work things out. But, she had counted on the baby to bring them closer together. Instead, it would only create more dissension. Probably he would want her to get an abortion, and by now she was determined to do no such thing. If they stayed together and had the baby, could he ever accept the child? Or, would he always be waiting and watching for some terrible sign-that the child would turn out like Alicia? And if the child had any faults, would he feel she was to blame? Would Dorothy herself keep feeling a sense of shame for "having bad blood?" And if she stayed, how could she keep her child away from Alicia and her destructive influence?

She must start completely over. She did not tell Stephen why in her note, only that she would be in touch about the legal arrangements.

She and Stephen had been friends with several couples in their apartment building but she did not go to any of them. She did not trust herself to say good-bye. If only one person tried to dissuade her, she might not be able to remain strong. Instead, she went to see a single friend whom Stephen had not met. He would not look for her there.

Her firm had wanted to send her to Arizona some months earlier, but she had refused. Stephen was not ready to move. Even though it was Saturday, she telephoned her boss at home. She was ready to be sent to Arizona. She told him only that she was getting a divorce and needed to go somewhere as far away as possible. The position she wanted was now filled, he told her. However, the boss had contacts with other firms in the Phoenix area, if she was really determined to go there. Perhaps he thought Stephen beat her. At any rate, he was sufficiently sympathetic to offer to make some calls for her. And, he promised that he would tell Stephen, if Stephen should ask, only that she had resigned. This was working out for the best, Dorothy decided. If she no longer worked for the same firm, she would be harder to find.

The lawyer was more difficult to deal with. He asked Dorothy to wait, to seek marriage counseling. She had made the mistake of telling him she was pregnant.

"If the judge finds out, he will not grant your divorce," her lawyer told her, "because even if a child is conceived in wedlock, it will be illegitimate if born after a divorce."

Sobered as she was by this news, Dorothy was still determined to go through with her plan. If she waited until the child was born, Stephen would have to know about it. Then there might be fights about custody. She would have to grant him visitation rights. And what if he took the child to his mother? Would she tell her grandchild about her "bad blood" on the other side of the family? No, her way was best. She would simply start life over.

When the lawyer was convinced that she wanted no alimony or child support, he agreed to handle her case and keep his mouth shut about the pregnancy. "But you're acting against my advice," he warned. She agreed to send him her box number when she arrived in Arizona.

Several days later she was on her way. The West, with its vast space and rugged landscape, offered new hope. The little flat-topped mesas, the more rugged purple mountains, and the huge cacti were so unlike anything Dorothy had ever seen that she felt her old identity was really slipping away. She found an apartment in a building with Spanish architecture and a sunny patio. Gradually, as the months passed, she added Navajo rugs and Indian artifacts. Her metamorphosis had begun.

Her new boss was not pleased that she was pregnant, but because she was so efficient, he could not really complain. When her baby was born, she missed only a week. Before long she was promoted.

She had written her father and brothers saying that she was getting a divorce, and for her own mental health she needed to stay away from Alicia. She would give them her box number in another town but not her address or the name of the business for which she worked. She did not mention the baby. Her father's first letters had been anguished and indignant. What had they done to deserve this treatment? Had she no sense of duty to family? Finally, he said he understood she must be upset over the divorce. They had been in contact with Stephen and he had had the nerve to say that Dorothy was unstable. Eventually her father had lapsed into a hurt silence, which lasted until the final plea before his death. She could not cut off her brothers so easily. Had she not been a second mother to them? On holidays she sometimes sent them money, and occasionally, they wrote her some news. They eventually gave up trying to understand her behavior and seemed to accept the situation. Alicia wrote Dorothy only once, saying, "I know this is all Stephen's fault-if you need me, I will help you..." The irony of it moved Dorothy to tears. The only person who did not condemn her was the source of all her troubles!

Shortly after Dorothy's arrival in Arizona, she had shed the names of "Deveroux" and "Smith." She chose "Foster" because it had been Aunt Patty's maiden name. When her baby girl was born, she, too, became a Foster. In a moment of weakness, she considered contacting Stephen. What would his reaction be? Had he finished his project and graduated? Was he now in love with someone like Susan? But the divorce papers had arrived at the post office box. She had signed them and sent them back. It was best to leave matters alone.

The new Dorothy thrived in the Arizona sunshine. With her newly-acquired tan, people thought she was part Spanish or Indian rather than part French, which she was. She now chose trendy clothes, with bolder colors than she had worn before. In the latest fashions, Dorothy's big bones were an asset rather than a liability. Although she might not be pretty in a traditional sense, she was striking in appearance. When dressed in clear reds, oranges, pinks and yellows, she caused heads to turn.

She worked as hard on her personality as she did on her appearance. Any signs of distrust must be rooted out. She deliberately cultivated an optimistic naivety, which she considered the opposite of paranoia. She refused to indulge in petty office gossip and said only the kindest things about her co-workers. On the surface, these qualities made her popular: her extreme fairness and rational decision-making ability worked to her advantage on the job.

Yet, at a personal level, she had problems. The relationships she had with the men she dated were superficial. One man even complained, "You are as cold and objective as those numbers you work with." On one level, Dorothy trusted everyone, but in the depths of her being, she trusted no one.

Baby Stephanie was a good baby who thrived in day care. Sometimes people would ask Dorothy, "Isn't it hard to care for a child alone? Don't you resent having to feed and dress your baby and take her to day care before you can come to work?"

For Dorothy, it was easy. Had she not, once upon a time, fed and dressed two babies before going to third grade? Now Stephanie was all she had in the world, and her care was more of a pleasure than a pain.

Most days their lives were serene. They enjoyed their Spanish style apartment, the swimming pool, the little outings to the park. But holidays were sometimes difficult. Dorothy envied her co-workers who went home for Thanksgiving, or those who cooked Christmas dinner for their husbands, children and other family members. As she and Stephanie ate their turkey alone one Christmas, she wondered: am I being fair to deny Stephanie an extended family? But then she remembered all the problems in her family and decided that loneliness was the lesser of the evils. Still, she felt some sadness when she recalled the few times she had enjoyed family holidays. On most occasions, Alicia's behavior spoiled things. But on several Christmases, at least, Alicia had behaved well and the family had been able to enjoy the holiday.

At other times, Dorothy worried whether having no father would harm Stephanie's psychological development. The little girl was approaching the age when she would begin to ask questions. Maybe, thought Dorothy, I should try harder to get interested in some of the men I know. And then the letter from Malcolm had come.

Chapter 17

IT WAS ON ONE OF THE EXTREMELY rare gray days in January that Arizona had, and Dorothy was feeling particularly bleak after the holiday season when she made her weekly trip into Phoenix to check her post office box. The letter from Malcolm made her heart leap. Twelve years ago he had promised to write.

For weeks, the fifteen-year-old Dorothy had walked to the mailbox each day, closing her eyes and putting her hand into the box. Each day she had been afraid to look-afraid that his letter would not be there. She was right. It never was. Later, her mother told her that Malcolm had been sent to a discipline school because Aunt Patty and Uncle Arthur couldn't control him. Her father said it was just a military boarding school to prepare him for college. Dorothy had decided that her mother was just being mean and telling lies again. But, she never heard from Malcolm.

This letter was very warm and friendly. Malcolm had finished his degree in business and was a salesman for some large corporation, he told her.

Since Uncle Arthur and Aunt Patty died, he continued, Dorothy's mother and father were all the family he had. He had been to visit them several times and was distressed that they had lost contact with her. No one seemed to understand why Dorothy had left, and did she know that her father was very ill?

In conclusion, Malcolm told her he was attending a sales meeting in Los Angeles the following week. He could stop over in Phoenix for a few hours on the way home. Would she come to the airport to see him? She need not reveal her address or any other secrets. They could have dinner and visit for old times' sake.

Of course Dorothy went. Not knowing whether or not she could trust Malcolm, she left Stephanie at home with a sitter. Malcolm might tell her family about the child.

In the end, however, she brought him home. She was still attracted to him. They had sat in the airport restaurant, exchanging bits of news. He told her that her father had Hodgkin's disease and was not responding well to chemotherapy. Her mother had had to go to the hospital for mental problems several times since Dorothy had left but was now living at Fox Hollow with the housekeeper that Aunt Patty had hired shortly before she died. "That housekeeper is a real sweetheart," he said with a grin. Dorothy knew he meant the opposite.

Malcolm also told her a little bit about her brothers' wives and Phillip's baby. Eventually, she felt secure enough to confide in him about Stephanie.

"No wonder you were so hurt you left," he said sympathetically.

How nice to find someone who understood! Malcolm, too, had been divorced. Married while in college, he had been so hurt he had dropped out when the relationship went sour. After several years of working, he had finally gone back and completed his degree. At least he did not condemn her for the divorce. He had been through the same experience himself.

Too soon it was time for him to leave. With a sense of panic, Dorothy realized that she did not want him to go again. "Couldn't you possibly stay longer?" she asked.

He could. "I do have a few days vacation coming," he said, "If someone were to invite me to visit, I could."

And so Malcolm changed his plane reservation for the following week. After leaving the ticket counter, he headed for the airport gift shop, where he bought the biggest stuffed animal there, a gift for Stephanie.

"One thing bothers me," said Dorothy on the way to her house. "Why didn't you write when we were kids?"

"I was stupid," he said, moving closer to her.

In a few days' time, Malcolm still did not leave. There was an angry telephone conversation with his boss in Louisiana. If he didn't return to his job, his supervisor said, he would be fired. After all, they had paid his way to attend a conference for a few days. They did not mean for him to take an extended vacation.

"OK, so I'm fired," Malcolm had said, and hung up the phone.

Dorothy could not understand his attitude. She had never been fired from a job. She had never missed work except for legitimate vacation days and the time when Stephanie was born. How could Malcolm be so casual? She assumed that he had an income from Uncle Arthur and Aunt Patty, yet she was concerned.

"Stop worrying," he told her. He had bought wine and had the grill ready to cook steaks. He had cooked every night after she got off work. "I was their best salesman, so I can find something else. The field is wide open."

"Besides," he asked meaningfully, "Aren't you flattered that I can't bear to leave you?"

She was flattered. She did not want Malcolm to leave. Probably he was right. There were a number of sales jobs advertised in the paper. She had no doubts about his ability to sell. He was not lacking in persuasiveness, and certainly he did not lack self-confidence.

The following day, as if to pacify her, Malcolm did look for work and seemed excited about several prospects. When he does find something definite, Dorothy thought, he will have to move out. Having a mother with a live-in lover was not the environment she wanted to provide for Stephanie. Unless, of course, he wanted to get married.

This, Dorothy decided, was what she really wanted-to marry Malcolm. She had convinced herself that she could not bear another unequal relationship where she was considered a liability rather than an asset. She could not bear the thought of loving a man who thought she was inferior, as Stephen and his mother had, because of a family situation she could not control. But wouldn't all men look down on her if they knew about her mother? Maybe that is why she had never let herself get close to anyone.

Malcolm did not look down on her. In a way, he was part of the same family. He knew about Alicia's illness. He knew that her brothers were irresponsible and had been in some minor scrapes with their misbehavior. He knew about her divorce and could sympathize, having been through a similar experience himself. He knew that Dorothy's former mother-in-law didn't want her to have a child. And he also knew that deep inside, Dorothy harbored a fear that she was genetically inferior and might some day end up like her mother.

He loved her anyway. He could accept her as she was. She would do anything he said!

While Dorothy was still in a quandary as to how to get Malcolm in the mood for marriage, the letter from her father had come. Without Malcolm she would not have been able to get through the following days-the conflict as to whether to protect her anonymity, to protect her new identity or to visit her father before he died could have torn her to pieces had Malcolm not been there. He was a solid rock, consoling her and easing her guilt. But, she must go, he felt. Otherwise, her conscience would not let her rest. After several days' procrastination, they decided that Dorothy and Stephanie would fly to save time. Malcolm would follow in Dorothy's car. And yet, they were all too late to see Dorothy's father alive.

Chapter 18

When Dorothy arrived back at Fox Hollow after looking at apartments, she felt she was in enemy territory once more. Her mother and Malcolm were both mad at her. Alicia was barricaded in her bedroom, and Malcolm was sulking at the dining room table as he pushed his limp broccoli around his plate with a soggy roll. Mrs. Crouch whispered to Dorothy that her mother had been difficult all day.

"After her fuss with you this morning, she said she had no one who cared for her," the housekeeper related. "She said she would just have to protect herself from everyone who was against her. So she had Mr. Phillip bring the gun."

"What gun?" Dorothy asked in alarm.

"The one Mr. Arthur left your father. Your father didn't think he should keep a gun with Miss Alicia being the way she was, so he left it at Mr. Phillip's house. Your mother has no business with a gun!"

"That's what I told Phillip," Malcolm condescended to speak for the first time. "But he brought it anyway."

Alicia, it seemed, had called Phillip and asked him for the gun. At first he refused, but after he got off work, he brought it.

While the housekeeper escaped to the kitchen to scrape up some of her unappetizing fare for Dorothy, Malcolm assumed an injured air.

"I ask a girl to marry me and she disappears," he said. "Not only that, you left me in such stimulating company. I don't know who is more exciting, your mother or Mrs...."

Before Malcolm could finish his sentence, there came the deafening retort of gunfire.

Guiltily, Malcolm half fell out of his chair, as though he thought Alicia had heard and was attacking him for the insult.

Running to the window, Dorothy saw her brother Scott's car careen to an abrupt and screeching halt in the curved drive. Another bullet ricocheted off its fender. Her mother was shooting at Scott!

Not knowing what to expect, Dorothy ran up the rectangular staircase, with Mrs. Crouch on her heels. At Alicia's bedroom door, they paused. Would she shoot at them too?

They had nothing to fear. Smiling happily and clutching the pistol, Alicia stood in the doorway, which led from her bedroom to the upstairs porch. If she had been angry at Dorothy earlier, she was now at peace, having just discharged her hostility in another direction.

"See. Dorothy," she said triumphantly, still waving the pistol. "You and I don't have to be afraid anymore. The person who wrote us those notes has been shown that we mean business. I will look out for you even if you don't care enough to protect me!"

"Miss Alicia, that's wicked. Put down that gun," Mrs. Crouch commanded.

Alicia's happiness faded momentarily, but then she clutched the gun to her bosom like a naughty child hoarding a toy.

"Nobody touches this gun but me. It was my husband's and now it belongs to me!"

"Mother, why did you want to hurt Scott?" Dorothy had now moved to the balcony and could see her brother crawling cautiously from the car. Malcolm was giving a helping hand and saying something like, "Your mother's gone completely crazy this time."

"Scott? It wasn't supposed to be Scott! It was supposed to be Harriet." Alicia's pleasure was fading. She looked confused and pathetic. Even though she could now see Scott, she refused to believe her eyes.

"I felt in my bones that Harriet was coming tonight. I have a sixth sense about those things, you know. Tonight she will come back," I said, "and I will be ready!"

"Mother, did you really want to kill Harriet?" Dorothy asked sadly.

"Kill her? Mercy, no! Didn't I just shoot at the fender and tire? I just wanted to teach her a lesson."

Alicia was telling the truth. Most of her shots had gone wild. The lower fender and tire were the only places on the car which were hit. But, wondered Dorothy, was the lack of damage due to Alicia's good aim or to her lack of it?

By this time, Scott and Malcolm had come upstairs. Alicia would not give anyone her gun, but Mrs. Crouch was able to persuade her to lock it in her dresser drawer. Dorothy noted that her mother put the key in her musical jewel box and vowed that she or Malcolm would come back and retrieve the gun while her mother was sleeping or out of the room.

"Mother, you really should get over your hatred of Harriet," Dorothy said, after Scott and Malcolm had gone to change poor Scott's tire, and Mrs. Crouch had returned to the kitchen. "You will do something you may regret. Harriet may not be your favorite person, but she doesn't deserve to be shot at."

"I make it a habit to never regret anything," Alicia answered petulantly. "And of course she deserves it or I wouldn't have done it, would I? It's a pity Scott got in the way, but if Harriet made me want to shoot her, then she must have something wrong with her," Alicia concluded.

As always, Alicia's brand of logic drove Dorothy into retreat. No one could ever, if one lived to be a hundred, hope to win an argument with Alicia, who first stated her hypothesis and then manufactured the facts needed to support it.

"All I can say is-you'd better watch yourself or you will find yourself in big trouble," Dorothy warned as she started out the door.

Feeling her mother's eyes on the back of her neck, she paused. Alicia was staring at her pensively, her blue eyes luminous.

"I always thought your Aunt Patty was sweet," she said in a hushed voice, "But she must have done something very wicked."

A cold chill gripped Dorothy. Involuntarily, she shuddered. "What do you mean?"

"Mrs. Crouch says that I may have done something to hurt Patty," Alicia said in a whiny child's voice. "If I did, that must mean that she deserved it. I wouldn't have hurt her unless she did something bad, would I?"

Sickened and revolted by Alicia's semi-admission of guilt, Dorothy slid out the door. Her mother's plaintive voice followed her down the hall. "But I could never remember what bad thing she must have done."

Inside her own room, she did not turn the light on. In the dark she leaned against the door, her heart pounding. What should be done about Alicia?

After a few seconds, she groped for her night gown. Mrs. Crouch must have thrown it in the wash, and Dorothy did not know where a clean one was. Reluctantly, she reached for a light switch. She had felt a moment's peace in the dark, but once the light illuminated the room, she screamed!

Chapter 19

TURNING, DOROTHY RAN DOWN THE HALL AND steps in absolute terror. She was being pursued by some malevolent force. Was it schizophrenia? She had come face to face with evil personified.

As the light had flooded her bedroom, she had taken a minute to focus her eyes, which had grown accustomed to the darkness. After blinking several times, her eyes had finally rested upon the large oil portrait in a tarnished metal frame. Propped upon her bureau, leaning against the stained and tattered rose wallpaper, was a portrait of her daughter, Stephanie. Yet the child's clothes were like none she had ever worn. Dressed in royal blue velvet with a cream- colored collar, the child seemed to have come from another era. Her clothes were like Alicia's; they had an inappropriate elegance, which did not belong to the real world. Raising her eyes to the painted Stephanie's face, Dorothy sucked in her breath in horror. Although the little girl's eyes were open, they were vacant. Her face was devoid of expression. It was as though the child might be mentally ill.

Beneath the picture lay a message, written once more in childish crayon. "Is this what you really want?"

But Dorothy's tormentor had more to offer. As her eyes traveled across the room to her bed, she saw the second portrait propped against her pillow. It, too, had a tarnished frame and appeared to have been painted years ago, judging from the cracks in the oil. In it, Dorothy once again, saw her little girl, Stephanie, this time lying in an open white coffin. The dead child's face had a look of tranquility. Perhaps the child was at peace because death had released her from her madness. Her dimpled hands clutched a small white prayer book, and at her head, a candle burned. Beside the child, in her coffin was a cream-colored velveteen rabbit with one eye missing. It was unlike anything Dorothy had ever seen. A second note lay beneath the frame. "Or is this what you would rather have happen?"

Mental illness is like an evil spirit, Dorothy thought. If it chose to come upon her, take her over, and destroy her, there was nothing she could do. How dare she think she could escape!

Yet she found herself running down the stairs, the evil spirit in pursuit. At the bottom of the stairs, coming in from helping Scott, Malcolm intercepted her.

Once in his arms, she could cry. Heading her into the back parlor where the phone was, he tried to make sense of her disjointed tale. "Something's wrong with Stephanie," she sobbed.

Lifting the telephone, Malcolm dialed Phillip's number. Phillip, not Carlotta, answered. Carlotta was out, he said. Dorothy would not calm down until she had talked to both Phillip and Stephanie. Nothing was wrong with the little girl except that she had to be awakened to talk to her mother. "I'm just nervous, I guess, because Mother has been shooting that gun. Why did you give it to her, anyway?" Dorothy asked.

After Dorothy had hung up, satisfied that Stephanie had not been harmed, she tried to explain to Malcolm about the portraits. He had brought her brandy, which she sipped gratefully.

"I want to keep Stephanie with me," she said, "but I can't keep her here, not while someone is playing those horrible tricks."

"It's your mother," Malcolm said. "You and I and Stephanie can live here without her and then the tricks will stop."

Dorothy looked at him mutely. She felt totally numb except for the burning sensation of brandy trickling down her throat. Malcolm was right, of course. Alicia would have to go to a hospital, even if she were not the one responsible for the tricks. She could not be allowed to go around shooting people. And what if she really had killed Aunt Patty? Dorothy did not even want to think about that.

Taking Malcolm's hand, she said, "Come on, I want to show you those pictures. If Alicia did this, she would have had to have had those pictures painted a long time ago-before Stephanie was even born. That's the part I don't understand."

"Did you have some relative who may have looked like Stephanie?" Malcolm asked, putting his arm around her for support. "Perhaps Alicia had an old family portrait that she used to scare you."

"I don't know of any relatives like that-at least none who died," Dorothy answered. "But I'm going to show Alicia those paintings anyway."

At her room door, she hesitated, feeling once more the fear she had experienced before. But now she was braver. Malcolm was beside her. Bursting into the room, she said, "There!" waving her hand dramatically toward the bureau and the bed. Malcolm's eyes followed her hand and then came back to meet her gaze. His face was a mixture of consternation and sympathy. The top of the bureau was empty and so was the space on her pillow against which one of the portraits had been propped!

"I don't understand," Dorothy stammered. They were both here. Look," she said suddenly, "the pillow has a dented mark where the picture frame lay."

"All that proves is that something was on the pillow," Malcolm said. "That mark could have been made by anything."

"But it was here! They both were!" Dorothy shrilled. She felt herself getting hysterical again. The spirit of evil was descending once more.

Malcolm took both her hands and made her sit down. "All of these things: your father's death, your mother's antics with that gun-all of this has been hard on your nerves," he said.

"You think I'm crazy like my mother," she accused, starting to cry again.

"Look, I'm not like your first husband. I don't care what kind of relatives you have. I want to marry you anyway. Why don't we get the license tomorrow? You'll feel better then."

She nodded mutely. She was lucky to have him. "But I don't want you to think I'm crazy."

"I don't pay any attention to that hereditary stuff," he said. "But if you have to keep living with Alicia, she might run you crazy. She would drive anyone crazy. So, once we're married, we'll get her committed to some nice home and we can take care of the place for her. We can even get this wallpaper fixed," he said with a smile.

It would be all right, Dorothy decided, for Malcolm and her to live here if her mother went to a hospital. They could do the repairs that were needed. But she wouldn't use her mother's money. They would live on their own income.

"Let's go first thing in the morning," she said, "We can be the first ones at the court house."

Malcolm grimaced. He hated to get up early. "But for that, I'll make the sacrifice," he said.

He would have stayed, but she chased him away. This house had too many people, supernatural and otherwise, snooping about for romance to flourish. But now she was no longer afraid. Exhausted, she fell asleep quickly.

Chapter 20

In the middle of the night, she was awakened by a sound. Sitting up in bed, she listened intently. A door had opened and closed. But when she opened her own door to peer out, the hall was empty and all bedroom doors were closed. A night light from the hall below cast just enough light for her to see. However, nothing was to be seen. Closing her own door, Dorothy reached reluctantly for the light switch. When the light came in, flooding the room, would she see those hateful portraits again? Or something even more horrible? For a few seconds, she kept her eyes squinted, afraid to focus them. When she did, she was relieved to note that the room was in order. No new surprises awaited her. Yet her curiosity about the portraits was heightened, if anything. Then her eyes rested upon the small door which led into an attic storage closet. As a child, she and her brothers had played hide and seek in there. It had a door which led through the attic into another room. Perhaps the portraits were old family ones and might be there yet. Whoever put them out and then removed them might have shoved them into the attic, or even carried them through the attic into Uncle Arthur and Aunt Patty's old room, no longer used. Cautiously, she opened the little door and peered inside. Several cartons of miscellaneous items were near the door, but no picture frames.

Gently, she tugged at one of the cartons, which seemed to be full of old books. With some effort, she slid it through the door into the room.

Trying not to be put off by the dust and musty smell, she opened several of the books, which had belonged to Aunt Patty. Her heart was warmed by the sight of Aunt Patty's handwriting. She did not feel she was snooping when she opened Aunt Patty's diary. It would be like a visit from her aunt, whom she sorely missed.

The diary had notations dating back some fifteen years. Most of the earliest notations were about social events she had enjoyed with Uncle Arthur. They had belonged to a country club and were friends with a group of people who had country homes in the area, like they did. Later, Dorothy was pleased to note that her aunt said nice things about her and her little brothers' visits. At one point, she had said, "Poor Alicia had to go away again. I don't know how Dorothy manages."

The next section was particularly interesting. "Because Arthur and I could not have children, we have always enjoyed doing things for our niece and nephews. But," she had continued, "I wonder if adopting a boy past sixteen was a mistake. Arthur and I can't seem to make an impression on him. I suppose that by sixteen, the character is already formed."

Dorothy was not unduly alarmed. Yes, Malcolm had been spoiled and somewhat brazen when she first met him. She supposed Aunt Patty spoiled him because his parents had died. He was still very appealing.

Later, Aunt Patty mentioned their decision to send Malcolm to military school because he played around too much in high school. They were afraid he wouldn't graduate if they didn't send him to a school with a stricter discipline code.

Well, Dorothy thought, still not perturbed, my own brothers were no great achievers in high school. And, at least Malcolm had finished college later. This was more than either Phillip or Scott had accomplished.

Dorothy read on, "We are lucky to have found Elsie Crouch to help us around the house. She is an old family friend who has fallen into hard times. She lived by Arthur's family a long time ago and even graduated from high school with his younger brother, Daniel."

That would be Dorothy's father. Dorothy had to chuckle. Mrs. Crouch and her father were classmates? Had she ever been a young girl? Or was she always wrinkled and dried up, perpetually frowning?

The diary continued: "Elsie may have been sweet on Daniel back then, but she married a man who drank and used her badly. Although never rich, Elsie came from respectable people. It's too bad to see how she's gone down. Life has not been kind to her. She seems to mean well, even if a bit eccentric…"

Later, Patty had written about Arthur's death, her loneliness, her efforts to cope through faith and prayer. She had decided to invite her husband's brother and his wife to move in.

Dorothy laid the diary down. She now felt like an intruder. The writing was now getting too personal, too painful.

Tiptoeing into the hall again, Dorothy had an inspiration. She would look for the portraits in her mother's room. She was now feeling quite strong and able to cope. None of the bedrooms at Fox Hollow had doors which locked. It was not difficult to silently turn Alicia's doorknob. For a moment, she hesitated. Would her mother awaken and shoot her? That wretched gun! How she despised guns! But, she remembered, the gun was locked up and the key was in the musical jewel box with the cherubs on top.

When a cursory glance around the room revealed no sign of the offending portraits, Dorothy decided to seize this opportunity to get the gun away from Alicia. Whatever pills Alicia was taking were doing their job. She was like a dead person. Hopefully, Dorothy felt along the dresser for the jewel box with the dancing cherubs on top. Whatever she did was wrong. Her touch set off the mainspring and a waltz began to tinkle as the cherubs danced about. Alicia moaned in her sleep and pulled her cover over her ear. She did not awaken. Bless that new doctor and his stronger pills, Dorothy thought. By this time, she had throttled the little cherubs into silence and secured the key. Stealthily, she slid it into the lock of the dresser drawer. The drawer stuck and once more Alicia stirred. After an agonizing moment and another squeak or two, Dorothy was able to get the drawer open wide enough to thrust her hand inside.

The drawer was empty!

Had someone been here before Dorothy? Was that the sound that had awakened her? Or, had Alicia outwitted them all again? Sometimes her mother was dumb like a fox. In her sleep, a little smile played around Alicia's lips. Was she awake even now and enjoying the scene? Possibly the gun was under her pillow. And if so, it would not do to startle her. Gently, Dorothy eased back out of the door. Something would have to be done about Alicia soon.

By now, the first rays of sunlight were streaming in the hall windows. Dorothy decided to dress and go make coffee. If she could beat Mrs. Crouch to the kitchen, she could escape the watery eggs, wheat germ cereal, or other health food delight that Mrs. Crouch might concoct. Although she dressed with care-she was going to get a marriage license, after all-she still was the first one in the kitchen. Before long, she had bacon frying, pancakes with butter and syrup, and fresh hot coffee. In a few minutes, she would awaken Malcolm.

Just as breakfast was almost ready, she was startled by a knock. Who would be here at this hour? She laid down her spatula and went into the front hall. There at the door stood her ex-husband. "I came to see my daughter," he said.

Chapter 21

Panic was her first reaction, but then she calmed herself. He's only bluffing, she thought. He suspects, but he doesn't know. I don't have to admit anything.

"Come on in, Stephen," she said with resignation. "You're looking well."

He really was. In college, he had been too thin. Now, he had filled out, and it became him. He also had been in the sun. Her compliment was sincere.

He returned the compliment with equal sincerity. "You've changed," he said.

To Dorothy, it was the nicest thing he could have said. When married to Stephen, she had been mousey and colorless, both inside and out. Today, dressed in a Mexican print of pinks and reds, she knew she was flamboyant.

She let him follow her into the kitchen, where she rescued the bacon from burning. She may as well offer him something, she thought. She could cook more for Malcolm. "Do you always go visiting at seven-thirty in the morning?" she asked. How much, she wondered, should she admit about Stephanie?

"I came on the way to work," he said, "I didn't want to put it off. But, I see you're up and dressed. You always were an early person. In fact," he continued in a critical voice, "you used to sneak out of the house before I was up."

She handed Stephen a plate and coffee cup, which he accepted with apparent gratitude. Taking her own, she moved into the dining room. Part of her hospitality was not motivated by courtesy. She was buying time to avoid a confrontation. Now, she could delay no longer.

"What gave you the idea you had a daughter?" she asked.

"You know I do, so just admit it."

"You obviously think you do, but I have a right to know why."

"All right,: he said. "Yesterday my mother went shopping at a mall, and while there, she saw my daughter."

"That's the most ridiculous thing I ever heard," Dorothy said. "Your mother saw a child and decided that it was your daughter. How could she possibly know that, even if it were true?"

"Because," he said, "that child was the image of my sister who died."

The sister! Of course. She was the child in the portrait. Forgetting all caution, Dorothy laid her hand on Stephen's arm.

"Please," she said, "you have to tell me something. Did your parents ever have any oil portraits painted-after your little sister was already dead?

"Oh God, yes! Those horrible things! But how did you know? They were destroyed years ago!"

A chill came over Dorothy. Was the appearance of the portraits a supernatural act? She shook off the feeling. "Tell me about them," she said. "Did your sister have a velveteen rabbit with only one eye?"

A look of sadness came over Stephen's face. "I was the one who pulled out that eye," he said. "My parents bought her that rabbit and I was jealous. I tried to take it away from her. When my parents made me give it back, I pulled out the eye. I thought if I made the rabbit ugly, she wouldn't want it anymore. But she loved it even more. She wouldn't sleep without her rabbit. And when she died, my parents thought it wasn't right for her to be without her rabbit…"

"But why," Dorothy probed gently. "Why did they want those portraits made? I should think they would have preferred to remember her living."

"They would have, if only they had made the portrait when she was alive," Stephen said, "but they had neglected to have any photographs or other portraits made. All they had were a few snapshots of her as a tiny infant."

Dorothy nodded. She could not remember seeing any baby pictures of Stephen's little sister, although she had seen some of him. This was the way parents were with second children, she supposed.

"Anyway," Stephen continued. "Mother had arranged to have her portrait painted on her third birthday. But, of course, she never had it. She drowned only a few days before."

"So they had the portraits done anyway?" Dorothy asked.

"Mother had the idea that if the painter could view the body, he could make the portrait appear alive. The body was not the problem. They propped her, dressed for burial, against a satin pillow. He had no trouble painting her hands, her dress, or her hair. The face was what gave him trouble. He tried to paint her as though she were still alive, but not ever having seen her alive, he couldn't get the expression right. Although her features were correct, the expression was bizarre. The result was hideous."

"I know," said Dorothy.

"Then the artist felt so badly he offered to do another one free. He said he felt it was wrong to paint a dead child as if she were still alive. He felt that my parents must accept the fact that she could never be brought back to life, even in a portrait. The second time, he painted her as she really was, and for that type of painting, it was better."

It was true, Dorothy thought. The little girl's face had seemed more at peace in her coffin.

"Did they like the second portrait better?" she asked.

"No, at least my father didn't," he answered. "He thought they both were hideous and ordered them destroyed. But my mother took them and put them in the back of her closet—I think I remember that now. I thought she had finally destroyed them, but she must not have done so."

Stephen went on to tell how his sister's death had led to his parents' divorce. Dorothy had never really heard some of these details before.

"But where did you see those paintings?" he demanded.

"Come on, I'll show you," Dorothy said, leading him up to her bedroom. "One was here, she said, pointing to the bureau, and one was on the bed. How could they have gotten from your mother's closet to my bedroom?"

Stephen was frowning, disturbed by what he heard, especially about the accompanying notes.

"If I could just show you," she lamented, "Then you would believe I really saw them."

"Maybe I can help you!"

Both Stephen and Dorothy whirled about, startled to hear Mrs. Crouch's voice at the door. How long had she been there-eavesdropping?

The housekeeper turned and picked up something that she had propped up in the hall. "These are what you are looking for," she said. "I heard you talking, so I went and got them."

The eerie pictures were not nearly so terrifying in broad daylight, especially now that Dorothy knew who the child was and how she had died. These portraits were merely pathetic-symbols of the parents' futile attempt to preserve the memory of a beloved child. Stephen, if anything, was more pained than Dorothy was at the sight of the portraits because of the memories they aroused. Dorothy could feel genuine sympathy for him and for his parents.

"She really does look like Stephanie," Dorothy said softly. "But how did these pictures get here?"

"I have a good idea," he answered thoughtfully, "but I can't say any more. Don't worry," he reassured her. "I'll tell you when it's appropriate."

It might be his mother, Dorothy thought, and that's why he won't say more. She would want me gone. Yet, Dorothy could not imagine Stephen's mother, who was always so dignified and formal, playing a trick of this sort.

"Mrs. Crouch, how did you come by these?" she demanded.

"I heard you scream last night, so I came up the back staircase just as you were running down the front one. When I went into your room and saw those strange portraits, I figured your mother was up to her tricks again. I waited a few minutes and then took the pictures and the notes into her room. I meant to confront her, but she was asleep, or pretending to be. I decided to put everything in my room and then confront her this morning."

"And you didn't know who the dead child was?"

"No."

A second thought occurred to Dorothy. "Did you, by any chance, take the gun when you were in my mother's room?"

"No, but we should do that. I was afraid she wasn't really sound asleep last night. We can wait until she's downstairs for breakfast. I will tell her I won't bring her tray"

"It's too late. She's already put it elsewhere."

As Mrs. Crouch went off downstairs, clucking her tongue over Alicia's misdeeds, Stephen brought the conversation back to the subject of his child. Dorothy saw no more need to deny Stephanie's existence. "You really do have a little girl."

"Where is she?" he wanted to know. "Let me see her."

"My brother, Phillip, and his wife, Carlotta, live in the house where my parents lived when you knew me. I left Stephanie there because of my parents' illnesses. I didn't know what I would find in this house when I returned from Arizona."

The revelation of Stephanie's whereabouts seemed to disturb Stephen even more. Probably he had hoped to see his child immediately.

"I don't know how you could have done this to me," he burst out. "It's incredible that I have a child nearly three years old and have never even seen her. You have robbed me of all those years!"

"I know," Dorothy said softly. For the first time, she felt she may have done wrong. "I'll let you see her. We'll work out some arrangement that's fair. I'll try to make it up to you."

"Excuse me! I hope I'm not interrupting something." She had forgotten all about Malcolm! "I've been looking everywhere for you," he said. "Mrs. Crouch said you had early company." He emphasized "early."

"This is my ex-husband, Stephen. Stephen, this is Malcolm."

Neither one said, "Pleased to meet you."

"I'm sure it would be fun to visit about old times," Malcolm said, "but Dorothy and I were just leaving. We're on our way to get our marriage license."

If congratulations were in order, Stephen did not offer them. Picking up the two portraits, he descended the stairs. "I hope you meant what you said about a fair visitation arrangement, Dorothy," he said in parting, "because if you didn't mean it, I will have to take legal action."

As the front door closed behind Stephen, Malcolm burst out, "If that creep thinks he's going to come dropping in over here after we're married, he has another think coming."

"Well, I suppose he'll have to come to pick up Stephanie. Unless," she added mischievously, "you'd rather I took her to his place."

"I just don't understand you, Dorothy. You moved to Arizona to keep your daughter away from Stephen, and then I hear you volunteering to let him visit her."

Moving toward him, Dorothy kissed him lightly. "Let's don't fight all the way to the license bureau," she said. "I couldn't help it if he showed up here. It's not like I invited him."

"All right," said Malcolm, putting his arm around her as they made their way out the front door, "but you have to admit that not too many men would be thrilled to see their intended bride entertaining an ex-husband in the bedroom at the crack of dawn."

Meaning to change the subject, Dorothy asked, "Did you ever get breakfast?"

"Mrs. Crouch gave me a bowl of something that stuck to my teeth," he grumbled. "It's strange," he added. "I could have sworn I smelled bacon frying when I first woke up."

Dorothy decided not to mention that she had fed the bacon to Stephen.

Chapter 22

AFTER APPLYING FOR THE MARRIAGE LICENSE AND completing the blood tests, Dorothy and Malcolm decided to visit the downtown store where Phillip worked. It was approaching noon and they could take him to lunch. Malcolm also wanted to go see his old employer about the possibility of returning to work. With a pang, Dorothy realized she would need to seek employment, too. She would need to find a good babysitter or nursery school for Stephanie. And, they would have to decide whether to live in an apartment or move to Fox Hollow. Malcolm had had an apartment before he left for California and Arizona, but had let his lease go when he decided to stay in Arizona. If they stayed in Fox Hollow, they would need to get her mother into a hospital. This decision was the one which troubled her most deeply. Was she doing the right thing for her mother, or were she and Malcolm just wanting to get Alicia out of the way? The marriage was to take place in three days, and some of these decisions would need to be made by that time.

The department store was one of the oldest and largest stores in town. After finding their way through the men's wear to the shoe department where Phillip worked and still not finding him, they inquired at personnel. He had already gone to lunch, they were told, They were also advised to stop by the book department. Phillip often stopped by there, the manager added, with a knowing look.

By looking across the arch beneath the escalator, they could see the book department. A girl with long brown hair appeared to be turning her cash register over to another clerk. Leaning against the counter, obviously waiting for her, was Phillip. Neither saw Dorothy or Malcolm approaching, and before they could get across the aisles, the girl had taken hold of Phillip's arm and walked away with him.

"What Carlotta said must be true!" Dorothy exclaimed. She decided not to run after her brother and the girl who so obviously had his attention. Did they walk arm-in arm to lunch every day?

Malcolm did not appear to be too shocked. "You know your brother is not trustworthy," he shrugged. "After all, he did get Carlotta pregnant before they married. That's why your father picked you to be responsible for your mother instead of your brothers."

A sickening thought occurred to Dorothy. Could Phillip have been responsible for the tricks which were being played? He had been at Fox Hollow on both occasions that the malicious notes were left. But how did he get his hands on the portraits? Perhaps he had been in touch with Stephen's mother. But what would be his motive?

Sadly, Dorothy realized that Phillip did have a motive for wanting her to go away. If he wanted to divorce Carlotta and marry the girl in the book department, he would need more money than he could earn selling shoes, especially if he had to pay alimony and child support. And, Dorothy realized with a heavy heart, she could understand why Phillip might feel he was entitled to be in charge of the family money. He had been the eldest while she was away for several years. She was sure he felt insulted that his father had not considered him worthy to have any money until Alicia was dead. And, even then, he would get a smaller portion than Dorothy.

She did not say anything more of her fears to Malcolm, but she resolved to talk to Phillip privately. If he could not afford a divorce, perhaps she could help him. On the one hand, she did not approve of his behavior. But on the other hand, she could understand why he might not be able to get along with Carlotta.

By the time Dorothy and Malcolm finished their errands, it was late afternoon. Malcolm's former boss had not been totally against hiring him back, possibly because Malcolm prevailed upon his sympathy. He had taken off work, he said, because of illness and death in the family. A firm commitment was not made but Malcolm was optimistic that his former boss would reconsider in his favor. Dorothy filled out some application forms but would not get interviews until later.

They could not agree on an apartment. Dorothy wanted to lease one for a short time. That way she could take Stephanie from Carlotta and Phillip's home and still not have to expose the child to life with Alicia at Fox Hollow. If Alicia were to be committed to a hospital later, then they could all move to Fox Hollow while she was away. Malcolm, on the other hand, wanted to move directly to Fox Hollow. He felt they could monitor Alicia's behavior more effectively if they were living in the same house and could recognize her need for help more quickly. Mrs. Crouch might not notify them soon enough if she did something dangerous-like shoot at someone again.

The decision would have to wait. Dorothy wanted to see her child.

Malcolm did not want to stop by Phillip and Carlotta's house. "It's getting late," he said. But Dorothy insisted.

Phillip, not Carlotta, came to the door. Malcolm seemed relieved that Carlotta was shopping. Phillip, however, was looking worried and the maid, Mattie, was crying! Stephanie had been kidnapped by her father!

"Mattie called me to come home," Phillip said. "Carlotta went out and we can't find her."

A sick feeling engulfed Dorothy. Stephen had seemed so humane, almost gentle, this morning. Until, of course, Malcolm had appeared and made his announcement about their marriage. Was Stephen that vengeful, that he would use Stephanie to hurt her?

Tearfully, Mattie related her story. A conscientious woman, she blamed herself. After the two children had taken their naps, she had dressed them and taken them into the front yard. Seating herself into a lounge chair on the front porch, Mattie had been holding Sara on her lap while Stephanie played with toys on the sidewalk. When the stranger had driven up, Mattie assumed he was a salesman or someone to see Phillip. Instead, the young man had informed her politely, but firmly, that he was going to take Stephanie with him.

"He say he the father of that girl," Mattie sniffed. "I say I don't know about no father, but he just pick her up and leave!"

Because she had been holding Sara, Mattie had not been able to move fast enough to physically hold on to Stephanie, and because of this, she blamed herself.

"That's some great guy you married," Malcolm commented sarcastically.

Dorothy was too upset to answer him. Part of her found comfort in the knowledge that Stephen would not physically harm Stephanie. But what about her mental health? What would she think-to be swept away by a strange man? And would she think her mother had abandoned her?

"Where would he take her?" she muttered. "Maybe to his mother's house. In a few seconds, she had dialed the number of her former mother-in-law.

"A lot has happened since I saw you last," Dorothy told her. "My concern is that Stephen has taken my daughter without my permission. Did he, by any chance, tell you where he was taking Stephanie?"

Mrs. Smith's answer was cool and guarded. "No, I didn't know he planned to take Stephanie away. But," she reminded Dorothy, "You must realize that the child belongs to Stephen, too. If he took her, he must have had a reason to do so."

Dorothy hung up in frustration. What had she expected? Probably, if Mrs. Smith had known anything, she would not have told Dorothy.

Dorothy's next move was to call the police. Their indifference to what they considered a family squabble further infuriated her.

"Lady, these parent-kid snatchings happen all the time. People get divorced and they fight over the kids. Often as not, the daddies get tired of them and bring them back And they seldom hurt their own kids."

All of this was small consolation to Dorothy. After some angry words, she did get the police to agree to watch both Stephen's apartment and his mother's house.

Hanging up the phone, Dorothy was near tears.

Phillip brought something to drink.

"I feel so helpless," Dorothy said. "I feel I should be doing something. I don't even know where Stephen works."

"Probably the police will find Stephanie in his apartment," Malcolm tried to console her. "Your ex is probably dumb enough to take her to his place."

"Dumb he isn't," Dorothy shot back. "But where else would he take her?"

"We can hire a private detective in the morning," Malcolm offered.

Dorothy was not hungry, but Malcolm welcomed some leftover supper that Phillip offered. "Mattie fixed this chicken for me earlier," he said.

"Didn't Carlotta come home for supper?" Dorothy asked. "The stores will be closing soon."

Phillip's face looked grim. "Carlotta goes and comes as she pleases," he said bitterly.

"Phillip, I know it's none of my business but we saw you today with another girl. We were going to take you to lunch but you were just leaving. Are you interested in this girl romantically?"

Phillip lowered his eyes. He was holding his daughter, Sara, who had fallen asleep, her head on his shoulder. "Yes," he said.

"Are you going to divorce Carlotta?"

Phillip sighed, "Probably not. At least not right away."

"Is it money you need?"

"That's part of the reason," he said, "but," he added, glancing toward the sleeping child, "it's not the only reason."

The baby, Dorothy thought. She is the reason he stays with Carlotta.

"Do you resent the fact that our father left me in charge of the money?"

Phillip looked uncomfortable. "I resent the fact he didn't trust me," he said. "But I don't envy you and the decisions that lie ahead of you. I wouldn't trade places with you."

"Honestly?"

"Honestly."

With a heavy heart, Dorothy parted with Phillip and allowed Malcolm to drive her to Fox Hollow. A feeling of numbness crept over her. She knew Malcolm was trying to be kind with his talk of hiring a detective and of prosecuting Stephen, but she could not respond with gratitude.

She felt inert, unable to move or to think clearly. All she ever wanted was a wholesome environment for Stephanie-the kind of family all children deserve-free from danger and with no eccentric or crazy relatives. Perhaps this was more than anyone could expect.

At Fox Hollow they were greeted by a hysterical Alicia and a distraught Mrs. Crouch. "Where have you been?" Alicia wailed. Someone had stolen her gun. She was sure some enemy was waiting, ready to pounce upon her.

Mrs. Crouch, on the other hand, felt Alicia had moved the gun herself and was "forgetting" its whereabouts just to be cantankerous.

Ordinarily, Dorothy would have been more upset. Was Mrs. Crouch the culprit after all? Might not the housekeeper be up to some murderous mischief? But Dorothy's own problems weighed so heavily upon her she could not feel concern for anything except her child. In a halting voice, she tried to tell her mother about Stephanie-about the pain and emptiness she was feeling. Perhaps Alicia would sympathize. She was, after all, a mother, too.

As always, her mother could not hear her. "I should think you would be more worried about the gun," Alicia said. "Someone might shoot us in our beds, and all you can do is whine about your quarrels with that no-good husband you once had. You don't care about me or my feelings."

Alicia was right. Dorothy did not care about Alicia or her feelings. She could not identify with the feelings of an egocentric person like her mother. And, Dorothy realized, her own pain was driving her to be just as egocentric. She and her mother were like two children- both absorbed totally in self.

In her room, the note awaited her. Numb as she was, Dorothy felt no surprise. Neither could she feel fear or anger. She had grown accustomed to the crayon-scribbled messages. They were becoming like old friends, familiar but evil companions leading her down the path to a predestined madness.

"You would not listen to me and do as you were told, so now you are getting what you deserve."

Chapter 23

SOME TIME IN THE NIGHT, SHE HEARD a bell ringing. She had been dreaming-first, that she had found Stephanie with Stephen on the steps of a church. The cloudless sky was blue and the air was crisp. The sun shone on a white cross. The bells of the church were pealing. Was it for her own wedding, or was it for Stephen and someone else? Or, was it for a funeral?

When she reached to touch her daughter, the child pulled away. "I don't like you any more. I just like my daddy now. You've gone crazy like my grandma."

Somehow, Dorothy had started to cry, but instead of a grown woman crying for her lost child, she was a child herself ringing her mother's bells and Alicia was saying, "It's your fault I am so nervous…"

Shaking herself awake, Dorothy realized that the ringing came from downstairs. Her mother had never had a phone installed upstairs. She was still in her clothes. She had not undressed for bed, thinking she could not sleep until she knew where Stephanie was. Yet she must have dozed off, fully dressed.

The hall clock said a quarter to one.

The phone had stopped, and when Dorothy turned to ascend the stairs, it began again. With a feeling of simultaneous fear and relief, she raised the receiver and heard Stephen's voice.

"I called earlier but your mother hung up on me," he said, "and when I called a little later, that Malcolm person started threatening me. He wouldn't call you to the phone, so I hung up on him."

"Where is Stephanie?" Dorothy gasped. "I want my daughter."

"I can't tell you where she is. But I do want you to know she's fine. I didn't do this to upset you."

Fine, thought Dorothy, he wants me to know his motives were pure. "Then why did you do it?" she asked weakly.

"There's something very wrong going on in your household," he said. "You said yourself that there was a missing gun. I wasn't sure Stephanie was safe in your custody."

That superiority again, Dorothy thought. Stephen's family looking down on hers. A helpless rage engulfed Dorothy. Because of her family, she was no longer a fit mother.

"Are you saying that I am unstable?" she asked softly.

"I don't know," he answered frankly. "When you ran away, I was sure you were. But I honestly don't know who or what you are now. I do know that several of your relatives may be dangerous."

"What are you planning to do?"

"Keep her until I know more about your situation."

"You won't get away with this. I'll fight you."

"I'll be back in touch," he said, "and Dorothy, please be careful."

Before she could answer, he had hung up. Sitting on the floor of the back parlor, she held the phone and cried. Was this the beginning of the end? Would Stephen take her to court and prove her unstable, using her mother as exhibit A? They must not commit her mother to a hospital right away, Dorothy decided suddenly. This action would just focus public attention on the family weakness. She must try to give the impression to everyone that Alicia was cured and not at all dangerous. Mrs. Crouch must be counseled to play down Alicia's erratic behavior in the event that Stephen raised the custody issue in court. In the morning she would tell Malcolm that they must move to an apartment, leaving Alicia in the care of Mrs. Crouch. Alicia's mental health must not become an issue until the custody of Stephanie was resolved to Dorothy's satisfaction.

With leaden limbs, she roused herself to go back upstairs. Once again in her room, she couldn't sleep. Kneeling beside the carton box of books, she reached for Aunt Patty's diary. Perhaps the words of her aunt might console her and lift the heavy weight of depression that had started to settle upon her. The brown leather book seemed lighter than before. As she lifted it, several pages fluttered to the floor. The spine had been broken and the pages were all loose. As she opened the book, Dorothy could see that the last pages of Aunt Patty's life had been removed!

Chapter 24

It was near dawn before Dorothy slept again, still in her clothes. She felt she had only just closed her eyes when she heard bells again. Rousing herself, she stumbled into the hall. The grandfather clock said a quarter to eight.

This time the doorbell was ringing. Although it was later than Dorothy had thought, it was still too early for most guests.

Stephen! It must be Stephen! Only he would come at this hour. Perhaps he was tired of running after a three-year-old. What was it the police sergeant had said? "Sometimes these kid-snatching daddies get sick of them and bring them back."

She opened the door to Carlotta. The black-haired woman looked haggard, less attractive than usual.

"I know it's early," she said, "but I wanted to get here before any of the busybodies got up. I'm going to help you get your daughter."

A feeling of hope surged through Dorothy's being. She had misjudged Carlotta. This woman was her friend, after all. Shaking off all lethargy, Dorothy ran to wash her face and run a comb through her hair.

"Don't take all day," hissed Carlotta. "I don't want to chit chat with any nosy people just now."

Who was it Carlotta didn't want to see? Dorothy wondered. Mrs. Crouch? Alicia? Or was it Malcolm? At the moment, she didn't care. She was going to see Stephanie.

Clutching her purse, she followed Carlotta to the car. Fox Hollow was surprisingly still in the morning sunlight. Even Mrs. Crouch had not been stirring.

Pulling out of the drive, Carlotta sped past the country club where Uncle Arthur and Aunt Patty had once belonged. "I used to belong there once upon a time," Carlotta said, with an edge in her voice. "Phillip thinks we can't afford it now."

Dorothy could understand. If Phillip had not been given his father's house free of payment, he probably would not be able to support the baby's nursemaid or Carlotta's shopping sprees.

"I used to wear only designer fashions," Carlotta went on, a metallic quality creeping into her voice. "Now Phillip thinks I should wear those sleazy things from that tacky store where he works, just because he gets a discount."

Dorothy did not want to hear about Carlotta's financial woes. And where was the woman taking her? They seemed to be nearing the neighborhood where Stephen's mother lived.

Abruptly, Carlotta pulled to a stop before a formidable white mansion. Clustered stone pillars around a curved front entrance gave it a highly formal effect.

"I was raised here," Carlotta said. "The people who live here now are so common they were voted down for membership into the country club.

"When I went to college, my father went bankrupt," Carlotta continued. "We lost the house."

"Where are your parents now?" Dorothy asked, impatient for Carlotta to finish her story and lead her to Stephanie.

"They live in a tacky trailer in some retirement village. They say they don't mind not having money. Well, I mind! They don't realize how much I mind!"

Dorothy ventured to bring up Stephanie again. Instead of answering, Carlotta turned on her. Her dark eyes were popping dangerously. With venom she spat out. "Phillip should have been in charge of your father's money! He stayed here while you ran off to Arizona. But then, you had to come back to get the money. I tried to warn you to leave, but you wouldn't listen, would you?"

The notes! So Carlotta was the writer of the crayon messages. Was this woman even more unbalanced than Alicia?

"You should have signed over your guardianship to Phillip and then gone back to Arizona," Carlotta continued. "Phillip and I could have enjoyed that money."

"Phillip told me he doesn't want the money," Dorothy replied.

"He doesn't have any sense. I would have made him take it."

"I know you wanted me to leave," said Dorothy, "but why did you write those notes in crayon, like a child?"

Carlotta had started the motor again. With a jerk, she pushed the car into gear and sped away.

"I wanted to disguise my writing," she said. "I hoped you'd think it was your mother," Carlotta added, with a voice of contempt. "That's the kind of thing she would do. I figured you'd be so disgusted with her that you wouldn't want to be around her. Then you'd turn her over to Phillip, and he'd be the executor of the estate. For a few days, I thought you'd really do it."

Dorothy thought back to the appearance of the notes. The first one had been in her room the night everyone was having dinner at Fox Hollow. Her mother had blamed Harriet, and Mrs. Crouch had blamed her mother. The second set of notes could have been brought by Carlotta when she and Phillip drove over to deliver her mother's gun. But the pictures? What of them?

"How did you get my mother-in-law's portraits?" she asked.

Carlotta laughed mirthlessly. "Oh, that! That was a stroke of luck. You threw me right into that woman's path when you asked me to get your daughter at the mall. When that Mrs. Smith told me that the little girl looked just like her own child who died, I just told her who Stephanie really was. "

That made sense, Dorothy thought. She had not been able to understand how Mrs. Smith could be so sure who Stephanie was on the basis of the child's looks alone.

"I told her you were unbalanced like your mother," Carlotta continued. "I told her you wanted to keep the child away from her and Stephen, but I would help her see Stephanie whenever she wanted."

Carlotta's car was speeding away across open country. They were heading away from the neighborhood of Stephen's mother. Where is she taking me? Dorothy wondered. And for what purpose?

"That mother-in-law invited me to come to her house that same day," Carlotta continued. "She showed me those portraits of her own kid. It gave me the idea of how to scare you. The woman played right into my hands. She even asked me to take the portraits and show them to you. She said she wanted to be reasonable and get along with you. She thought the pictures might soften your heart and help you to see that she would love Stephanie."

Dorothy knew the rest of the story. While she had been hunting apartments, Carlotta had gone along to Fox Hollow with Phillip and sneaked the portraits into Dorothy's room. The last note, of course, had been placed at Fox Hollow while Dorothy and Malcolm were away, probably at Phillip's house, when Carlotta had supposedly been out shopping.

One piece of the puzzle was missing. "Why did you write a note to my mother?" she asked. "If you wanted me to think my mother did this, why did you do the same thing to her?"

Carlotta frowned. "I didn't. Someone else is trying to run your mother crazy. Crazier than she already is, I mean."

"And it's not you?"

"Why would it be me? As long as you have control of the money, I want to keep the old bat sane! If you put her in a mental home, then you and Malcolm will just marry and move into Fox Hollow, and Phillip and I will never get a chance at anything. Oh, I know, Phillip is supposed to get a fourth when Alicia dies, but Malcolm will find a way to spend everything before then. I've been trying to encourage the old biddy and be kind to her so she'll keep her wits about her."

That was true, Dorothy knew. Carlotta had been uncharacteristically kind to Alicia since Dorothy's father's death.

"I didn't want Alicia to go crazy too soon," Carlotta continued, "that would just make life too easy for you and Malcolm. After Phillip and I take over her guardianship, the old bat can either go crazy or die-I don't care which; she can take her pick!"

"After Phillip and I take over…" What was Carlotta plotting to do with her?

They were on the freeway. Carlotta's small car was careening dangerously around the curves.

"What do you have in mind now?" Dorothy asked, wondering if Carlotta was also the person who removed Alicia's gun. "What does this have to do with Stephanie?"

"Stephen and his mother trust me," she said. "I met him briefly at her house. They were grateful that I had told them the truth about your daughter."

"I can get her for you," she continued. "I will tell them I'm taking the kid for ice cream or something. They are indebted to me because I told them I would testify against you in a custody hearing."

Carlotta had now pulled up in front of a low building, which housed legal offices. Was there some litigation about Stephanie already in motion, she wondered. She felt both dread and relief. She was relieved that Carlotta had not pulled a gun on her or gone off the road with her crazy driving, but she, nevertheless, dreaded to hear what the woman was plotting next. "Are Stephen and Stephanie here?" she asked in a small voice.

"Oh no," answered her sister-in-law with a sneer. "Your former husband said that since you kept Stephanie from him for three years, he was going to have his turn now. If you behave yourself, he might let you visit your daughter when she's six."

"I don't believe Stephen is that cruel."

"You'd better believe it, Honey. He and his mother are going to initiate custody proceedings on the grounds that you are unstable, and also, if you live near your mother, she would be a definite threat to the child!"

"They don't have any evidence against me. It won't hold up."

"It will when I get up in court and tell some cute little stories of child abuse-how you didn't want to be bothered with your child and left her at my house all these days."

"Why would you do that? What do you want from me?"

"Honey, I thought you'd never ask."

"The money, you want my father's estate in exchange for my daughter."

"Aren't we clever? You do have a brain after all. I was beginning to wonder what you had between your ears. I flunked high school math, but I'm light years ahead of you, Honey. Neither you nor your brother would have the sense to go to the bathroom if someone didn't lead you to it."

The crude insult was not important to Dorothy. She just wanted her daughter. "Tell me what to do."

"I thought you'd never ask THAT, either," Carlotta gloated. "You are going to walk into that office and talk to your father's lawyer. You are going to tell him you cannot accept the terms of your father's will. Your executive powers are contingent upon your willingness to assume responsibility for your mother. Tell him you are emotionally unable to fulfill your responsibility for Alicia and you want your brother Phillip to do it."

"You might recommend that Scott get his fourth of the estate when Alicia dies," Carlotta added as an afterthought. "If he doesn't, he might bother us about it. But don't ask for anything for yourself. That will leave three fourths for Phillip."

"You have to get my daughter back first."

"Uh, uh. I call the shots now. You don't have any say-so. You do as I say and I'll take you home. Then I'll go where Stephen has hidden your daughter. I'll tell him she has to have her shoes exchanged or something. Then I'll call you to meet us at the ice cream store. You can hide in the restroom in case Stephen insists on coming along with me and the kid. He won't be able to follow us into the bathroom. You can snatch her while I distract Stephen, if he's there, and then you can go straight to Arizona. You could have your suitcase in the car. He wouldn't be able to find you there. He has no idea where you live and he doesn't know you changed your name."

"I'll do it," said Dorothy. Wasn't this what she really wanted anyway? To take Stephanie and return to Arizona? If Malcolm wanted her, he could follow her there. She never wanted the money anyway. And she definitely had never wanted to be the guardian of her mother. Carlotta was right in one respect. She was not emotionally strong enough to deal with Alicia objectively. Phillip would be better. Only a day or two earlier, she would have made this same decision on her own. Yet now she felt weak and spineless, allowing Carlotta to insult her and push her around. Still, she could not risk a court battle with Stephen. Even worse, he might keep Stephanie hidden away forever.

As though she were sleepwalking, Dorothy opened the side door and slid out of the small car. Carlotta crossed over to her side and stayed close on her heel.

"I'm coming with you to make sure you do it right," she hissed. "Don't try anything cute if you want to see Stephanie again."

Woodenly, Dorothy entered the corridor and found her way to Mr. Snyder's door. The receptionist seated them in the empty waiting room. The lawyer had just come in and they were his first clients of the morning. Carlotta had called ahead the day before, saying she was making the appointment at Dorothy's request.

At first, it seemed that he would resist Carlotta's plan, presented by Dorothy as her own idea.

In a halting voice, Dorothy had told Mr. Snyder that she had not known what her father planned to do-that he expected her to give up her job and her home in Arizona to come care for her mother. Now she was finding herself emotionally unable to cope with the situation.

The lawyer looked stern. "All of us would like to walk away from our responsibilities at times," he said. "Dorothy, I knew your father. I know that he trusted you to take care of your mother."

Dorothy began to tremble. She was beginning to feel physically ill.

"We don't just change a will on a whim." Mr. Snyder continued. "Should you decide that you absolutely cannot be responsible, then the courts would have to decide who should be responsible for your mother."

"But my husband and I want to help Dorothy," Carlotta chimed in. "We want to take the responsibility off her shoulders."

The lawyer looked sharply at Carlotta and then at Dorothy. Noticing how pale and shaky Dorothy had become, he took a kinder approach. "I suppose Phillip would be the logical person to do this, Dorothy. I can probably draw up a document for both of you to sign and let the court review it, provided both parties are willing."

"I can take it to Phillip to sign," volunteered Carlotta.

"I want to see him in person," the lawyer said, peering sternly over his glasses.

"Today?" Carlotta asked brightly.

"Tomorrow will be soon enough. I don't have time today."

"But Dorothy wants to go back to Arizona to her job."

"She will have to wait," the lawyer said, dismissing them.

As she and Carlotta left the office, Dorothy's spirits sank. This messy business would take at least twenty-four more hours. "I kept my part of the bargain, so go get Stephanie now," she challenged Carlotta.

"You'll have to wait a day on Stephanie. I can't let you grab her and take off until this job is done. Besides, you aren't finished. You have to go down to Phillip's store and convince that brother of yours to take both the money and your mother off your hands."

"What if he won't?"

"He will if you convince him he's doing it for your sake. And you'd better if you ever want to see your kid again."

Some of the shock and numbness was leaving Dorothy. She was more lucid now. What if she told Phillip the truth about Carlotta's scheme? What would he do? Or, maybe she could call Malcolm and have him trail Carlotta when she left Dorothy at home.

"I need to call Malcolm and tell him where I am," she told Carlotta.

"All right, but don't tell him what's going on. Tell him we're shopping for your wedding dress," she said with a mirthless laugh.

The two women stopped in a coffee shop with a pay phone. Dorothy dropped her dimes in and dialed Fox Hollow. After several rings, she heard Mrs. Crouch's voice. The woman sounded under a strain.

"Your mother's terribly upset," she said.

Alicia had been crying and saying that she felt she needed to be punished for having murdered Aunt Patty. Although Alicia could not remember anything about the circumstances of Patty's death, her guilt over the event was becoming an obsession.

"Malcolm had called her psychiatrist. He wants to take her to the hospital and let the doctor evaluate her.," said Mrs. Crouch, "but I'm afraid all this talk of murder will get your mother in trouble with the law."

This would never do! No matter how disturbed Alicia might be, they must not draw attention to it at this time, particularly if she were babbling about murder. Any notoriety or family scandal would just help Stephen win custody, in the event that Carlotta was not able to snatch Stephanie back from him.

"Let me talk to Malcolm," she said.

In a minute he was on the line.

"I don't know where you disappeared to," he said, "but your mother is worse. I'm taking her to see her doctor."

"No, Malcolm, you can't do that!" Dorothy protested. "It's absolutely essential that no one know that my mother is worse right now."

"Dorothy, you're stalling. You know you are too tender-hearted to put your mother in the hospital, so you've got to let me do it for you."

"You can't do it. I'm the one who is legally in charge of her."

"Are you saying your will block me-that you won't give consent?"

"That is exactly what I'm saying," Dorothy snapped. Noting that Carlotta was glaring at her, monitoring her every word, she said, "I can't explain why, but Malcolm, we cannot let my mother go into the hospital for a long time-not for several weeks or months. I mean it."

Abruptly, the phone went dead. Had he hung up on her-or was the phone disconnected?

Turning to Carlotta, she said, "Malcolm's getting ready to commit Mother to a hospital. We've go to stop him. This business with Phillip can wait until he gets off work."

Carlotta, oddly enough, agreed. Probably she felt that Phillip's chances for getting control of the estate would be better if Alicia were not in the midst of some mental crisis. "I want to keep the old bat sane until I in control," she had said.

Speeding away once more, the two women arrived at Fox Hollow within a half hour. Dorothy's car was gone and so was Mrs. Crouch's. Were they too late?

Chapter 25

THE FRONT DOOR WAS UNLOCKED AND THEY let themselves in. The downstairs was deserted. Climbing the stairs, they found Alicia in the middle of her room, her hair tousled and her face streaked from crying. She wore her frothy pink net and nylon negligee that she had worn on the first night of Dorothy's return, the one with pink rosebuds embroidered on it.

"I have to be punished," she said, looking directly at them. "I am bad and I need to be punished."

"Where's Malcolm? And Mrs. Crouch?"

"Mrs. Crouch had to go buy my medicine. She thought Malcolm was going to stay with me, but after she left, he took off, too."

"He was going to take me to my doctor," Alicia continued. "Maybe you can do it?" she asked with pathetic hope.

"You don't need a doctor; you're just fine, Alicia," Carlotta encouraged her mother -in-law with false cheer.

What a hypocrite! thought Dorothy. But at least Malcolm had not dragged her mother to a hospital. She must get Stephanie back before she allowed that to happen.

Carlotta agreed to go, having satisfied herself that Alicia was alone in the house. "We'll both talk to Phillip tonight," she said to Dorothy on the way out,, "but remember, if you can't convince Phillip to go along with this plan, I won't raise a finger to help you get your kid. In fact, I'll see to it that you don't ever get her!"

Closing the door behind her obnoxious sister-in-law, Dorothy heaved a sigh of relief. Were it not for Stephanie's sake, she would never tolerate the presence of this odious woman again. Now she must deal with Alicia's crisis; she must try to calm her down.

Her mother was now sitting on the edge of the bed, her pink nylon net draped over her like a bridal train. She reminded Dorothy of a queen holding court. Yet her countenance had a penitent and humble expression.

"I want you to believe me," she pleaded, as Dorothy reentered the room. "I never meant to hurt Patty. I never meant to do any of the bad things I've done."

"Then why did you do it? Especially to Patty?"

Tears were beginning to fall again. Alicia dabbed at her eyes with torn bits of tissue.

"I don't remember," she said. "I try and try but I just can't remember." Turning her eyes toward Dorothy, she added plaintively, "You must believe I never wanted to be the way I am. When I was young everyone loved me," she continued. "Your father was the only person who still cared after I got sick. When I was little, I had the lead in the Christmas play and everyone said how pretty I was. In high school, I had nine boyfriends. But nothing lasts, does it?"

Once more Dorothy was struck by the incongruity of the scene. Here sat a delicate Southern lady, adorned in pink rosebuds, with the mind of a child. Surrounding her were the objects of love: the glass case of tinkling bells, the beautiful furniture, the ceramic birds. Yet in all probability these innocent baubles were the toys of a murderess, the play pretties of one who had done evil. Letting her eyes rest on the bureau, Dorothy noticed her mother's music box adorned with the dancing cherubs, the ones Dorothy had strangled into silence. Yet in the drawer beneath these innocent cherubic faces, her mother had laid a deadly weapon.

The gun! Where was it? What was it Phillip had said, the reason why he brought it here? The gun was no longer in that drawer. The gun was in the mirror now. And there was a hand attached!

Hurtling herself full force, Dorothy knocked her mother off the bed before the glass in the mirror shattered. They rolled together across the floor. Half dragging her mother through broken glass, Dorothy crept into the hall as their would-be killers' footsteps echoed on the upstairs porch.

They were not safe in any room, Dorothy knew. Because all of the upstairs rooms had windows opening onto the upper veranda, they would be vulnerable and exposed everywhere.

The hall linen closet would be their salvation. Quickly, Dorothy pushed Alicia ahead of her and slipped in behind her. The linen closet was the walk-in kind with shelves for towels and sheets above, and space for dirty laundry below. Alicia and Dorothy could both huddle in this space until they were sure the killer was gone. Here, they would be out of the line of gunfire.

The footsteps had seemed to be going away, yet Dorothy waited for what seemed to her an agonizing long time before pushing the door open a crack. On the floor of the linen closet was a laundry chute, which had once been used to send soiled laundry to the basement. Someone had obviously mistaken the trap door for a trash bin because some scraps of paper were stuck in the flap. They were some missing pages to Aunt Patty's diary!

"I don't understand you, Dorothy," Alicia complained. "I am the one who is supposed to be crazy. Yet here we are about to be shot, and you take a notion to sit and read."

Dorothy folded the papers and put them in her pocket. She was overcome with grief stronger than any she had ever known. This time the grief was for her own loss of innocence. She was not the same person she had been a few minutes ago.

Cautioning Alicia to stay hidden in the closet, she promised to slip downstairs and try to use the phone. It would be better to enter the back parlor through the kitchen hall, as the front staircase was more exposed to all the verandas, and the killer might still be lurking there.

Yet as she slipped down the back staircase, she knew what would await her in the pantry at the bottom. She knew but she kept going, just as a young girl she had approached that same dark pantry with both joy and dread.

When she was fifteen, he had used both arms to hold her while he kissed her. Now he kissed her with some tenderness a final time. But he only held her with one arm. He had to use his other arm to hold the gun. She fancied she saw the hint of tears in his eyes. At least he had the decency to be sorry. Her own tears were for her loss of love, not for what she knew was going to happen to her. The ultimate hurt was already done.

"You shouldn't have made me do this, Dorothy," he said. "But I no longer have a choice. You know too much."

In her pocket, the diary told the story. Aunt Patty had related how Malcolm came to visit-how he had been disappointed to be left out of Uncle Arthur's will.

"Arthur left everything to me and then to Daniel and Alicia when I die," Aunt Patty had written. "He was so upset when Malcolm divorced that nice girl and dropped out of school. He said he would leave enough for Malcolm to finish his education but no more. The boy didn't deserve it."

"Personally, I felt sorry for Malcolm," Aunt Patty had written. "He asked me if I would leave something to him if Uncle Daniel and Aunt Alicia were both dead. I said I would because Malcolm wasn't any worse than Alicia's boys. Daniel wasn't expected to live long, but Alicia needed the money if she lived. So I told Malcolm that Alicia would need the money as long as she lived, but I would consider him if she died."

"Why did you kill Aunt Patty?" Dorothy asked.

Malcolm's eyes still glistened. "I wouldn't have done it. I loved Aunt Patty. She was the only person who was ever good to me. Uncle Arthur was too strict, and my own parents didn't really care for me. Aunt Patty would have given me the estate, but your mother stood in the way. I knew your dad had Hodgkin's Disease and wouldn't last more than a year or two. If it weren't for Alicia, Aunt Patty would have willed everything to me."

"I belong at Fox Hollow," he said. "I always dreamed I would live here forever. It's the only real home I ever had. It should have been mine. Aunt Patty would have given it to me."

"Then why did you kill her?" Dorothy persisted.

"Your mother and father had just moved in. I knew she and Patty both liked their afternoon tea. I did my chemistry homework and found out which of their medicines would be lethal if combined. I thought I could just doctor your mother's tea so it looked like she had overdosed herself. But I didn't dare put more than just tranquilizers in the common teapot. The sleeping capsules I undid and dumped the powder into the sugar bowl. I saw that nosy Mrs. Crouch watching and I wanted to be sure she didn't see me touch Alicia's cup. She did testify later that Alicia had fixed her own tea."

"But you forgot my mother didn't like sugar," Dorothy said.

"That's right. Your mother dumped in half the sugar bowl and then gave the cup to Patty." Malcolm continued. "As soon as Alicia started to fix her tea I left and said I was going to the store. I didn't want to be anywhere near when it happened. According to Mrs. Crouch, Alicia said, 'Here, Patty dear, here's your tea-nice and sweet the way you like it. I don't take sugar in mine.'"

"Imagine how I felt when I returned later and found Patty in a coma, not Alicia.. Because of Alicia, I ended up killing the one person I ever loved. And because of Alicia, I have to kill the second one, too. You and Patty were the only ones I ever loved."

His hand tensed on the gun, even as the other hand was still caressing her head.

"But Carlotta-didn't she love you, too?"

"Carlotta never loved anyone but herself."

Aunt Patty's diary had said, "Malcolm brought his latest girlfriend to see us. Although she is the daughter of our dear friends, she has always been a spoiled and selfish girl. I'm afraid she only likes Malcolm because she thinks he is going to inherit my money. And Malcolm only liked her until he realized her parents were bankrupt. Unfortunately, he has gotten her pregnant…"

"I knew Baby Sara looked like someone in the family," Dorothy said sadly, but it never occurred to me she was your child."

Malcolm closed his eyes. The vein in his temple was throbbing and beads of perspiration were on his brow. The gun still rested against Dorothy's middle, as innocently as though it were a toy. But any minute now, he would feel compelled to pull the trigger.

"When Carlotta told me she was pregnant, I thought Aunt Patty would give me a lot of money to marry her. After all, she was a friend's daughter. Her parents used to belong to the same country club as Arthur and Patty. I know Aunt Patty would have wanted to help me if she hadn't died. But when Alicia switched that cup of tea, I saw no hope of getting Fox Hollow. I told Carlotta to get your brother drunk, seduce him, and make him think the baby was his. I thought Phillip would be the one to control the estate when your father died and your mother became incapacitated. Carlotta may have been crazy about me but she was crazier about money, so she did as I told her. She was supposed to funnel some of that money to me and let me live at

Fox Hollow, and eventually she would find a way to dump Phillip and come back to me."

Moving closer to her, Malcolm tightened his grip. The gun was becoming painful against her ribs. Malcolm's breath was hot on her neck.

"But it's your fault, Dorothy. It didn't have to be this way. I would rather have you than Carlotta, but you wouldn't cooperate."

"When my father told you he was leaving me in charge of everything instead of Phillip, you came to Arizona," Dorothy accused him. "And I thought you just wanted to see me for old times' sake."

"I did have a meeting in Los Angeles," Malcolm said, "And my intention was to use you to get back the inheritance that was rightfully mine. But then when I saw you, I really did fall in love with you.

"After all your mother had done to hurt you, I thought you would jump at the chance to send her to a mental hospital. You and I could have lived here at Fox Hollow and fixed it up the way it should be. We could had had a guaranteed income and belonged at the country club. We could have traveled anywhere we wanted."

If he moves any closer, I will suffocate, thought Dorothy. Would he kiss her one more time, she wondered, before he pulled the trigger?

"I realized this morning that you will never put your mother in a home. And even though neither of us wants to live with her, you will never do anything to her because you feel guilty you don't love her enough.

"I decided I'd have to kill her," he continued, "but you came in and saw me. I had planned to say she did it to herself. I sent Mrs. Crouch away to buy Alicia's medicine and I also gave her a long list of groceries and other things to get. I drove your car to a nearby garage to get the oil changed and told the guy I would be eating at a café until it was done. I walked quickly back to the house, was going to shoot Alicia and then get back to the garage. If Mrs. Crouch came back, she would see

I was still gone. But you had to come home too soon. You came into the room and saw me."

"We could still make it work, Dorothy," he said, half-pleading. "We could say she had an accident. Everyone knows how crazy Alicia acted with that gun. But you won't do that, will you?" he said, noting the expression of horror on her face. "You have to have morals."

She heard the click and knew he had released the safety catch. "You and Aunt Patty were the only ones I ever loved. It's a pity you have morals-that's why you have to die. I could have made you happy…"

A sound in the stairwell caused Malcolm to turn aside suddenly. The gun discharged with a deafening crash, but it was no longer pointed into Dorothy's ribs. Something heavy and filmy toppled on top of both of them, knocking them down.

Dorothy partially supported her mother's weight and saw a dark stain oozing through the pink net. Warm and sticky, it covered Dorothy's hand. With her head partially supported on Dorothy's knee, Alicia gasped, "I hope this makes up for it, Dorothy, for whatever bad thing I must have done…"

Chapter 26

Malcolm, momentarily stunned by what had happened, did not see where the gun had slid behind him on the kitchen floor. Moving quickly, Dorothy was able to retrieve it. By the time Malcolm looked up, Dorothy was standing halfway across the room, pointing the pistol directly at him. The crumpled and bloody form of Alicia lay stretched out between them. She had evidently crept out of the linen closet and had been listening in the upper stairwell before deciding to make the ultimate sacrifice of hurtling herself down the stairs between Malcolm and Dorothy.

Squinting, Dorothy checked the safety catch and took aim. Was it better to aim for his head or his heart? Could she bear to squeeze the trigger?

Rising from his knees, Malcolm was once again pleading, "You know I wouldn't have killed you, Dorothy. I loved you too much to ever do that. I just wanted to scare you and make you listen to reason about your mother. I only meant to scare her too, so she would want to go to a hospital."

"You are the one who convinced Phillip to bring this gun here. I remember now what he said on the telephone. You told him Alicia's nerves would be better with protection in the house."

"I only wanted to reassure her," Malcolm said softly, edging toward her-"But when I saw how crazy she acted with it, I decided to take it away from her while she slept." He had been the one, Dorothy now realized, to creep into her mother's room ahead of her and remove the gun.

"No, Malcolm, you hoped she would do something crazy with the gun so you could use it as evidence of her mental condition," Dorothy said. "You even hoped she would shoot herself. And when she didn't, you decided you would help her along with that chore."

Dorothy knew that she must act quickly. In a minute Malcolm would spring toward her. If he regained control of the gun, he would shoot her. She no longer cherished any illusions about him.

Her determination to escape her mother's fate, to keep herself free from paranoia, had made her too vulnerable. Her openness, her willingness to believe in others, had made her an object of contempt for those who had no morals. The ruthless, like Carlotta and Malcolm, only understood power-those who had it were worthy and those who did not were scorned as fools who deserved their fate.

He would kill her and lay the blame on Alicia. The coroner's verdict would be murder-suicide.

His face would be better. It would be quicker. But should she shoot in the eye or between them? With bloody and sweaty fingers, she started to squeeze.

"We can still make it, Dorothy. You and I," he pleaded. "Mrs. Crouch knows your mother was depressed this morning. I'll tell everyone it was suicide. You and I still have each other."

Was this the choice I must make throughout my life? Dorothy wondered-to be evil or to be weak?

Whirling suddenly, she ran out the kitchen door down the sloping ground toward the bayou. The gun was slimy with blood and sweat, metallic and slippery in her hand. She would not use the hateful weapon, even on Malcolm. Half crying and gasping for breath, she waded through the spongy grass and heaved the gun into the bayou. The odious weapon would do no more harm.

Malcolm, she hoped, would use this opportunity to run out the front door and escape. She knew he would have to be caught and punished. But let someone else bring him to justice.

"You shouldn't have done that, Dorothy. The gun would have been easier." He came up behind her and made a lunge.

Dear God, what would he do now? Hold her head under water? And then say she drowned herself? Without hesitating, she did a shallow dive into the murky, muddy water. Using a breast stroke, she pulled herself into deeper water, away from the shore and away from Malcolm.

The cool, murky water, green with algae, closed in over her head. Above her the sunlight filtered down, making golden streaks in the water. Below her in the algae were dozens of shimmering shapes. She knew she had dived into a nest of water moccasins. She did not care. If they killed her, it would be an impersonal act of nature-not like the betrayal of a loved one. The snakes had no malice. Only people were evil. She seemed to synchronize her swimming strokes with the movements of the moccasins. She felt almost in harmony with them and with all of nature. Gradually, their shadows fell away from beneath her. As a child, she had heard that moccasins do not strike in deep water. It must have been true.

Around the bend of the tree-lined shore was an unpainted shanty belonging to a man who had acted as an occasional caretaker at Fox Hollow. Gaunt and eccentric, Thomas Shaw was a male counterpart of Mrs. Crouch. Perhaps he would help. Emerging from the slimy water, Dorothy hurried to the door of the shack. The door opened, but the person she saw was not Thomas, the caretaker. It was Stephen! "Help me!" she gasped. "Malcolm is trying kill me!"

"Thank God you're all right," he said. Later, when asked why he should care, he said, "I don't know. I shouldn't have cared but I did."

Stephen had met Thomas Shaw, the caretaker, and had persuaded him to snoop around and find out what was going on at Fox Hollow. Leaving Stephanie safe with a friend, he had come to the caretaker's dwelling to see what he could find out about the activities at Fox Hollow.

When Dorothy and Stephen called the sheriff, Dorothy had learned that Mrs. Crouch had also just called them. She had returned from buying Alicia's medicine and groceries and found her mistress on the kitchen floor. Although an ambulance had been summoned for Alicia, it was too late to help her. She was still on the floor when Dorothy and Stephen got back to the house.

Stretched on the kitchen floor in her filmy gown of pink, Alicia looked once more like a young girl. This time the expression of peace and innocence which graced her countenance was deserved. She had died bravely like the fox Uncle Arthur had once seen. And she had died to save a daughter who never understood her. Only the blood which stained her embroidered rosebuds and satin ribbons suggested an incongruity in the scene.

Had Alicia been intentionally evil? Or was she an inhabitant of another time and place-a dweller, like Alice in Wonderland, of a fairy tale world-a world where other people could not go? Certainly, Alicia, who was mentally ill, had not done the evil things that the legally sane Carlotta and Malcolm had done.

While Dorothy's father had tried to protect Alicia from herself and to excuse his wife's every action on the basis of her mental illness, Mrs. Crouch had taken the opposite approach. Tearfully, she confessed to Dorothy that she had written the one crayoned note sent to Alicia. Mrs. Crouch's harsh life, her abuse by her husband and her poverty-level existence, had made this frugal, conservative woman attracted to a religious denomination which was more harsh than most churches. Her beliefs stressed the bad side of human nature and repentance for one's sins, including confessions of wickedness.

Mrs. Crouch was devoted to the Deveroux family, having once fancied herself in love with Dorothy's father, but she felt that Alicia's problems were due to her own selfish and stubborn nature. (Dorothy had shared some of this same belief, she realized.) Mrs. Crouch honestly believed she could best serve the Deveroux family by shaming Alicia into becoming a better person.

"But I was wrong, "she confessed. "I was so sure Miss Alicia had killed Miss Patty, not on purpose, maybe, but I knew she did it because I saw her dump all that sugar into Patty's tea. Whenever Miss Alicia acted up, I would remind her that I knew something on her. I was afraid she would do something worse if I didn't control her."

As she had admitted, Miss Crouch, not Carlotta, had written the crayoned note to Alicia "to pay her back for writing those notes to you and to teach her a lesson."

"I shouldn't have done it," she sniffed. "I just made her worse. She wasn't as wicked as I thought."

Or as I thought, Dorothy agreed silently.

"It's hard to say what you should have done, or what we all should have done," Dorothy consoled her. "Alicia had not the capacity to identify with other people's feelings. She was incapable of understanding any point of view but her own-yet in the end she sensed her own deficiency and reached out to try to make things right."

As her aunt and uncle had once said, "There was never a person exactly like Alicia." And there never would be again.

As they waited for the ambulance to take Alicia away, Thomas Shaw came in to tell them that he had encountered Malcolm, hobbling painfully away from the bayou with snakebites on each leg. Although taken to a hospital, he died the same day.

Chapter 27

Dorothy's car stood packed and waiting in the drive of Fox Hollow. She and Stephanie lingered to say good-bye to Stephen. Her three weeks' leave was almost over, and she would be returning to her job in Arizona.

After that terrible day when both Alicia and Malcolm died, Stephen had brought Stephanie back. Several times he tried to reassure Dorothy that he had not kidnapped the child to cause her pain when he had taken her to a friend's house, but to keep Stephanie away from possible danger.

"I met Carlotta at my mother's," he said. "And I knew she was treacherous because of the way she was double crossing you. And then when I saw how she used my dead sister's portraits to hurt you, I knew she was not a person I wanted to be around my daughter. But I couldn't insist that you keep Stephanie at Fox Hollow because I knew you were worried about your mother's erratic behavior, particularly the way she handled the gun."

Dorothy understood. If she had not been so determined to keep Stephanie from Stephen, he would have been able to take the child with her permission. And, she thought, if Stephen could have expressed his feelings three years ago the way he was doing lately, they need not have parted.

"I still don't understand why you didn't even want me to know about Stephanie," he had said.

"If only you could understand how it feels to be in a family with a mentally ill person," she had answered. "I felt so helpless-there was nothing I could do to make myself acceptable except to deny my membership in this family. I wanted a totally new identity."

"I felt that way once," he had said. "After my parents divorced, I felt it was somehow my fault. Actually, they blamed each other for my sister's death, but I always felt that because of that, I wasn't as good as other people."

"Everyone has something to live down," Dorothy sighed. "But I didn't want Stephanie to have any burdens like this. I didn't ever want her to have any relatives that had something wrong with them."

"Isn't that unrealistic?" Stephen asked. "You didn't have it that way and neither did I."

"If only you knew how I wanted to protect her, " Dorothy went on. "I wanted her to have the perfect environment."

He studied her thoughtfully. "Can anybody ever-really?"

Dorothy lowered her eyes under his gaze. "I guess Stephanie will have to take her chances like anyone else. She will have to just live and be whatever she is." At least she has two parents who care, Dorothy thought.

"I'm glad Phillip has decided to keep Carlotta's baby," she said. "If she didn't have Phillip, she wouldn't have anyone."

Dorothy had presumed, after Carlotta had been arrested for extortion, that Phillip would place the baby in a foster home. After all, it must have been a shock to discover that the child he thought was his was really Malcolm's. But Phillip did not react the way Dorothy expected.

"I've known all along she wasn't mine," he said, "But legally, she is my daughter and no one needs to know otherwise."

The lawyer, Mr. Snyder, had contacted Dorothy and told her that the original will was still in effect. "The suggested changes would have to be reviewed," he said, "and I knew from your behavior that day that this woman, Carlotta, had some kind of hold on you." When Mr. Snyder heard the full story about Carlotta's threatening to lie in court concerning Dorothy's child unless Dorothy gave up her rights in the will, he suggested Dorothy prosecute Carlotta. Dorothy was following this advice, not to get revenge but to help Phillip prove Carlotta was not a fit mother. In addition, Phillip threatened to accuse Carlotta of conspiracy with Malcolm to murder Alicia unless she relinquished custody of Sara. Although Carlotta was not really involved in Alicia's death, she had known about and approved of Malcolm's first attempt on Alicia, ending in Patty's death. Carlotta was not very interested in custody of her child anyway, now that the child was no longer seen as a means to manipulate Phillip and get wealth. Malcolm's death had hurt Carlotta deeply. Selfish as she was, she had been in love with him. No wonder she had despised Dorothy so.

Phillip had explained to Dorothy that Sara was the reason he had not divorced Carlotta sooner. Although he always suspected the child was not his, he had become attached to her.

"Carlotta had no maternal instinct," he said. "That baby could scream for hours and she wouldn't go near her. I finally realized that if the poor infant was going to survive, I would have to do everything for her. I had to hire a nursemaid to be sure the baby was looked after while I went to work. "

Phillip had never been responsible for anyone in his life, and the experience of looking after this tiny, helpless creature had changed him.

"One night I got up to feed her," he said. "And she reached out and grabbed hold of my finger. She must have been about five months old at that time," he continued. "I was the only person in the world who even cared if this baby lived or died. I promised myself I would never abandon her."

Dorothy understood. In her own childhood, she could not have abandoned her little brothers. She felt she was keeping them alive while their mother, because of her illness, neglected them. Phillip, like Dorothy, had a sense of responsibility.

He had offered to take custody of the child if Carlotta wanted a divorce, but Carlotta, anticipating family money, didn't want one. She had also used his affection for Sara to get her own way-threatening to take the baby away and abuse her if Phillip didn't give in during their arguments. This would all be changed now.

"Are you going to marry the girl in the book department?" Dorothy had asked him. "You have enough money now."

"Maybe," he answered. Phillip, like Scott, would have one fourth of the family money. He was happy to be getting it, but for the time being, he would keep the same job and house and provide for his daughter, the daughter who was more rightfully his than anyone else's.

Scott and Harriet, with their share of the money, were going to buy a franchise to a restaurant. Harriet planned to serve customers along with the other waitresses.

"I love waiting tables," she said. "Meeting the public turns me on."

"But if you are your own boss, you can rest when your feet hurt,' Dorothy reminded her.

"That's the best part," Harriet happily agreed. She was also going to take a dancing class.

"But not exotic dancing," Scott reminded her.

As far as her own part of the family money, Dorothy was making plans to invest it in Fox Hollow. She had promised to give a small pension to Mrs. Crouch, who planned to live with her sister, but the majority of funds would go to convert the large home into a facility for the treatment of emotionally disturbed children. She remembered the time while visiting her mother at a state hospital, she had been saddened to see children on the same floor of the mental ward as adults. "There are not enough facilities just for children," Dorothy had been told when she asked about the little girl who talked to herself-the one who was afraid of dogs.

She could never be happy living at Fox Hollow, Dorothy knew. Too many memories, both happy and tragic, would haunt her there: Aunt Patty's guest room, the back pantry, the kitchen with its gingerbread, the kitchen with it bloodstained floor. Malcolm kissing her on the back staircase, Malcolm with his gun in her ribs, still on the back staircase. Her brothers were happily settled elsewhere and did not want Fox Hollow for a home. Why not let it become a center for children? In cooperation with the local mental health association, she arranged to contribute funds for this cause. And in the front hall of Fox Hollow would hang a portrait of Alicia as a young girl, pretty and smiling with yellow hair and a yellow dress, Alicia as she was when admired by all as she recited in school plays.

Dorothy was leaving Fox Hollow feeling sad, but she was not depressed. Stephen was coming to visit her and Stephanie next month when he had some vacation days. He now had a good engineering position, having completed his degree shortly after the divorce. The blonde girl who had helped him with his project had been only a friend. She had married someone else.

Dorothy also knew she would be coming back to visit her brothers and to keep up with her mental health project at Fox Hollow. She would also probably have to go to court when Carlotta's case came up. Perhaps one day, as Stephen had suggested, they might eventually live at the same address, but both wanted to take the relationship very slowly. Whatever happened, she and Stephanie would survive. Smiling, she thought of the people she knew-the people in her office, her boss, her brothers, the people on the street; each probably carried some secret sorrow, if it could be known. Maybe this was what it meant to be human. She would no longer need to feel inferior. She would just live and be herself, a self she now could accept and like. Someday Stephanie would do the same.

She drove down the drive past the moss-covered oaks and magnolia trees. Looking back, Dorothy was happy to notice that the faded black and white sign at the entrance of Fox Hollow had been replaced with a shiny new one.

About the Author

WHEN JO ELLEN OLIVER WAS IN HIGH school, she won an Atlantic Monthly scholarship for her writing. She has a PhD in education and a master's in counseling. She has been a teacher and a counselor and is the author of one book, The Man Under the Bridge. Her pen name is Jillian Wright. Her husband, John, has written veterinary texts, and one son, Mike, is a newspaper editor. Oliver is the mother of three and the grandmother of ten.